Requiem For a Favoured Few

Paul Reid

EsteemWorld Publications
United Kingdom

REQUIEM FOR A FAVOURED FEW

Copyright © 2011 Paul Reid

ISBN: 978-1-907011-18-4

Published in the United Kingdom by
EsteemWorld Publications

British Library Cataloguing In Publication Data
A Record of this Publication is available from the British Library.

For further information or permission, address:
EsteemWorld Publications
United Kingdom.
E-mail: info@esteemworldpublications.com
www.esteemworldpublications.com

Printed in Great Britain for EsteemWorld Publications

For

Finola

1

A small grey haired man, in his mid fifties, walked out of the Blackrock Clinic in south Dublin. He turned right at the entrance and at the traffic lights, crossed a main southern artery to Dublin's suburbs. He then walked the hundred yards to the public park. He needed time and space to think.

He had been given the news by his consultant and it was not good. The tests had shown that the cancer was rampant and there was little to be done other than to provide relief from the pain. Time was uncertain. He had weeks rather than months to live, certainly not years.

He had had a good life. He had been successful and he had enjoyed the trappings of his lucrative career. His family had grown up and were now independent of him.

His wife had died some years before and there had been nobody else. He was tired. He would not be sorry to join her. He saw little point in waiting out the days and hours that remained, for the inevitable to happen. It would be easier for everyone if he went now. He did not want his children to see him shrink into a shell and have them relive the agony of their mother's illness.

Yes, it would be better all round if he went quickly. He had most of his affairs in order but there was something still to be done.

Nothing was going to schedule for Chief Superintendent Donal Joyce. He had been delayed in traffic and ended up being at his desk late and that was only the beginning.

It was close to ten o'clock before he got to his post. There were memos from police headquarters, notes from solicitors and communications from citizens on a variety of different issues. This time there was one item out of the ordinary.

The letter was addressed to him personally. It carried no address and was unsigned. The envelope was postmarked the previous day.

It read.

'By the time you read this, I will have terminated my life. This act has no connection with the contents of this letter. It is the result of a diagnosis of terminal cancer.

I realise that not much credibility is given to unsigned correspondence but I have a family and I do not wish to bequeath to them the legacy of a sordid and criminal incident in my life.

More than thirty years ago a medical student was found dead in a ditch on the road between Kilmacanogue and Roundwood. Her name was Joanne Boylan and she had been murdered. The newspapers at the time reported that little progress was ever made in the investigation. No one was ever charged with the killing.

The memory of what occurred on that night has remained with me all through the years. For the sake of my family, I did nothing about it. I realise that sounds weak but it is the truth, at least as I see it.

It was a pointless death. A group of friends, including myself, had been in the bar of the International Hotel in Bray, where Joanne Boylan worked and during the course of the evening, a lot of drink was consumed.

At one stage the conversation turned to achievements and what the gathered group considered to be the ultimate attainment. All kinds of ideas were flouted, ideas that seemed bright and courageous in the alcoholic haze of the night. Then somebody suggested the perfect murder. He defined a perfect murder as a killing where the perpetrator's identity never became known to the police. It needed to be a killing without motive. The reasoning was that a motive provides a link between the killer and the victim. The individual in question pointed out Joanne Boylan. He said that if one of the group killed her, there wouldn't be any connection between them therefore the killer would not be a suspect. No suspect, no charge, no conviction, therefore, the perfect crime.

Nobody took this dissertation seriously. The night continued and the crowd eventually retired to a nearby club. The group broke up at the disco and we all went our different ways.

Later, on leaving the club with two others, my friend, who had spoken of a perfect killing, was waiting outside. I will call him Dennis. Moments later, another of the group joined us. Dennis told us he had something to show us, so we went with him.

He took us to a deserted cul de sac near the disco and led us to a car parked, at the end of the lane. With a flourish, he opened the boot door and there we saw the body of Joanne Boylan.

It was madness and we told him so, but Dennis insisted that we were all involved and that he needed help to complete the scheme. In our shock we accepted what he said, and we all fully participated in the disposal of the remains.

The car had been stolen and, with the girl laid out in the boot, Dennis drove up into the hills towards Roundwood. One of us accompanied him, the others followed in my car, well to be strictly accurate my mother's car. When we got to the location where she was discovered we laid the body on the ground at the side of the road. Then all five of us, together, lifted her over a thick hedge into a ditch. And that was it.

I don't think all five of us ever socialised together after that night. We were never again the close friends we had been.

Who, you will wonder, are the others? I will give you one name only. That name is Dennis Hogan. I am referring to the current government minister. I believe he is the killer and it's this belief that prompts me to name him. I did not see him kill the girl and cannot prove he is the killer but it is my firm belief that the girl died at his hands.

I will provide you with one other piece of information which might prove useful if, as I hope, the case is revisited.

All five of us stood looking at the dead girl as she lay, face up, in the ditch. Hogan emptied his jacket pockets of their contents and threw the sports coat over the dead girl's face.

The car, that Hogan had stolen, was taken to Wexford. It was abandoned somewhere near Rosslare Harbour.

There was no more.

Joyce sat back and read the letter a second time. The Chief Superintendent, in the course of his career, had encountered false confessions on several occasions. He had also encountered confessions from people in search of redemption for past misdeeds. However, he had never encountered somebody confessing to a crime thirty years after the incident. Maybe others had.

Donal Joyce didn't know what he was going to do with this information. Was it appropriate to re-open a long unsolved case? Justice told him that any year is a good year to catch a killer. Budgets say no. He knew that after such a long period of time the chances of making a charge, let alone securing a conviction, were slim.

He would think about it, but he knew that it would be a waste of time. A policeman's duty is to battle crime and render unto the courts those in need of justice. As for the budgets, he would leave those to the politicians and the accountants.

There was only one thing that needed clearance and that was jurisdiction. But, if he wanted the case, he couldn't see the Bray station causing a fuss. Donal Joyce knew why he wanted it. He had been one of two young gardaí, just out of Templemore and stationed in Bray, who had been among the first gardaí to arrive at the scene near Roundwood.

The Chief Superintendent allowed himself a smile. He knew who he was going to assign to the case.

2

Harry Tinto sat at his desk. He was at his ease. His most recent case had been completed and all he and his team were doing was tidying up the pieces. Harry hoped there might be a short break before the next assignment.

Harry had fully recovered from his bypass surgery and had successfully closed a couple of cases since his return to work. He was aware that he would never be back to what he once was but he knew that and he was careful about his health. Emer and his three daughters made sure of that.

The last case had been a breeze. Sure, it was murder but there was no mystery about it. It was clear from the outset who was responsible. It was routine, collect the evidence and take care not to contaminate it. All told it was completed in a few weeks. Domestic disputes were always a canter but he didn't like those cases. They didn't stretch him. They didn't use his intellect or the skills he had built up over the years. To some extent he didn't see these cases as murder because, in most of them, there was no intent on killing. Matters just got out of hand through drink or drugs, passion or anger and somebody was dead. They were more manslaughter cases but it was not his role to make judgements or distinctions.

The phone rang, it was Joyce. He wanted to see Harry that afternoon at three o'clock. The Chief Superintendent gave no hint as to what he wanted but Harry could guess. There was to be no period of grace.

A few months before, Harry had been given a case involving the death of a young woman. Due to enormous pressure on the resources of the force to find the killer of five clerics, he had investigated the killing with a skeleton team. Afterwards, he had kept them together.

One of them was Emer Ryan. In the short time since Harry had met Emer, a personal relationship had developed and flourished. They were now a couple.

Emer had had a difficult summer. She discovered that her somewhat estranged son, who lived in London, was gay and she found this difficult. Why she found it so hard to accept she didn't know, but it was a disappointment.

Since Brian had graduated she had seen little of him. He had gone to London almost immediately and they met only occasionally in the intervening years. However, she was wise enough to know that her reaction to her son's orientation would be a determining factor in their future relationship and she had taken the bull by the horns and invited him and his friend to Dublin for a weekend.

She was amazed at the alacrity with which the invitation had been taken up and just two weeks later she was introduced to Michael. To her surprise Michael was neither English nor foreign but a lad from Athlone. Emer learned that they had been friends from their college days. What surprised her most was that she never suspected anything.

Harry was disappointed that Joyce was assigning him to a new case immediately. He wanted to take Emer away. He hadn't told her. It was to be a surprise.

'Harry, take a seat,' Joyce said as Harry entered, 'you finished the Lucan killing in jig time.'

'There really wasn't much to it, a domestic row that boiled over.'

Donal Joyce said nothing for a few moments.

'You remember Harry, when we were stationed in Bray. There was, you will recall, the killing of a young girl. We were among first gardaí on the scene.'

Harry remembered the case vividly. It was the first time he had been close to a murder investigation. Not that he was close but he was a serving officer in the same station and he remembered the disappointment he had felt when the investigation came to nothing. No clues, no evidence, no arrest and no conviction.

'Yes, the young girl, I think she was twenty. She was found in a ditch beside the road up the mountains,' Harry said. 'What made you remember that case?'

9

'This did.'

The senior policeman handed the letter, that he had received, over to Harry.

'Have a read of this, and then tell me what you think and what you feel I should do about it.'

Harry read through the letter a couple of times before handing it back.

'The choice, I have Harry, is between justice and budgets. They rarely work on the same side of the street.'

Harry Tinto knew his friend's predicament. After thirty years it would be a hellish job to get a conviction, so why try? But Harry knew it was not how Joyce worked.

Neither was it Tinto's way.

'What I'm going to do is give it to you and the small team you run. No resources other than the five of you and you'll have two weeks to assess the possibilities and then we'll talk again. That is Harry, if you want it. You can pass.'

'You know I can't pass,' Harry smiled. 'A fortnight is enough to tell us whether there is anywhere to go.'

For the next half hour the two friends talked of their memories of the case. They knew that there was nothing of value in their reminiscences but they enjoyed recalling those days when both were young.

Harry was pleased as he walked down the stairs to his office. His plan for a holiday with Emer had, for a time being, been relegated to a lower league. This case was a challenge he would savour. It would require intelligence and graft, good judgement and a lot of luck if anything was to come of the exercise. It would be a contest worth competing in, a duel of champions. Tinto and his small band of gladiators pitted against the mighty Hun.

Apart from himself and Emer Ryan, the other players on his team were Pete Halpin, Dan McCarthy and Billy Lynch. Dan was young but he was learning fast and would one day be a very fine officer. Pete was steady. Give him a job and he'd do it and do it well but he was not very good at taking the initiative. Billy Lynch was an old timer like Harry. They went back to the beginning together, just like Joyce. Billy was down for retirement at the end of the year.

When seated at his desk Harry re-read the letter that Joyce had given him. Harry figured there were three strands of detail that could be extracted from the document. First the writer, he was possibly recently deceased however that was by no means certain. There are many who plan their own death but in the end don't proceed with it. A guess might suggest a Dublin address because of the reference to the Blackrock Clinic. Whether the correspondent was male or female there was no clue but another guess would suggest a male.

The reference to cancer would be of help only if the informant had died. If he was still alive, there would be no help from hospitals or oncologists. Maybe the cancer diagnosis was just a red herring to throw the gardaí off the scent. But that scenario didn't make sense. If the identity of the group of drinkers was established then so would the writer's.

The next strand was the detail of the crime scene and without the research it was not possible to determine how much of it was first hand knowledge and how much was from reported material. The jacket was interesting of course. Thirty years ago it could hardly harm a suspect's defence unless it could be absolutely linked to him. Now it was different. With DNA such a gesture would send the perpetrator to Mountjoy for life.

Finally there was Dennis Hogan, the politician.

Harry sighed. This would be the second time in a few months that a case involving a government member was in his lap. He didn't think that the Taoiseach, Matt Dolan, would welcome him uninvited to Government buildings again.

This would to be a very different kind of case to anything that he had ever been involved with previously. It was unknown that an unsolved killing was resurrected after thirty years and a new attempt made to bring justice to the victim.

Harry's approach needed to be different. There was no crime scene to be examined. The location, where the body was found, no longer held any secrets for him and his team to find. The scene of the actual killing had never been established. Whether he could build a case sufficiently strong enough to make a charge was, in his opinion, remote. However, nothing ventured, nothing gained.

He would think about it overnight and inform his team of their new assignment in the morning.

'Well, we have a new case.' Harry announced to his assembled crew.

'The body of a young woman was found in a ditch between Bray and Roundwood.'

Although he remembered very little of the detail of the initial investigation, Harry gave a brief outline of what he knew to have happened all those years ago. He told them how a young student, working as a barperson for the summer, was found dead in a ditch up near Roundwood. It had been established that she had died elsewhere and that the body had been dumped there. No motive had ever been established. There had been no rows, no enemies. There had been nothing to go on and very quickly the investigation had petered out. The case had never been officially closed but no work had been done on it during the intervening years.

Billy Lynch interrupted.

'One question, Harry. Why us? It's not in our division.'

Harry stretched back on his chair and smiled.

'You are perfectly right, Billy. It's in the Bray division. New information has become available and Joyce wants to run with it and so do I. Why us, Billy? Well, nobody else wants it.'

Harry told them about the document that Joyce had received the day before. It was an unsigned testimony from a dying man. A confession from a man who was involved on the periphery of a heinous crime committed three decades before. Probably a good man, who had harboured a guilt throughout his life and now, as it was about to end, he wanted to clear the air and do what was right. Maybe do what he wished he had done when he had been young. Harry told them that the letter had contained a name and had accused that person of being involved in the killing Joanne Boylan.

However, for the moment, he was not going to divulge the name. Sooner rather than later they would need to know but for the present the identity of the accused was to remain his information.

Harry then distributed among the team copies of the confession with Dennis Hogan's name deleted. He wanted each of them to examine and study it. He would want to know their individual reactions to it later.

The first task to be done was to acquire what information there was from the original investigation. Harry and Billy would go to Bray. However, what was still available after thirty years was altogether another matter. How had it been stored? Where had it been housed? Had it been kept at all? Who knows what the answers were?

What might still be there, apart from the jacket, Harry had no idea. This was key information. Thirty years before, if the pockets had been emptied, there was little the technical people could examine, maybe fibres and blood but not much else.

But, with DNA, the jacket could be the means of putting the ruthless killer behind bars. Sure, it was late in the day but didn't someone once say that any day was a good day for justice to be done.

Chief Superintendent Matt Hynes was expecting them. He had not been sorry that his colleague had wanted the case. His men were hard pushed as it was and he had no desire to take on something that stood an excellent chance of going nowhere. It wasn't that he was against re-opening the case because he was in favour of it. He believed strongly that nobody should get away with murder and he would give Tinto all the assistance and co-operation that he could.

By the time Harry arrived in Bray, Hynes's people had tracked down much of what remained from the Boylan case. There were several old box files, discoloured by time and encrusted with dust. There were also two cardboard boxes warped by the years and tied with strings.

It had taken an officer several hours to find the treasure. They didn't think there was anything else but they would search again in the afternoon.

It was still only eleven o'clock when the car was loaded and Harry thought that a look at where the body had been found would do Billy and himself no harm. He knew the spot well. Over the years when he had passed that way, usually with his family on a trip to Glendalough, he remembered Joanne Boylan lying in the ditch behind the roadside hedge.

Following Harry's directions the driver had no difficulty finding the location. It looked ordinary, just as they expected it to look, a deserted stretch of road about eight miles from Bray. It probably looked no different from the night Joanne Boylan had been dumped there.

Later that day, the squad gathered with the material that had been collected in Bray. It would take a little time to get all the reports, not only logged but read. They would look at the contents of the boxes.

Here, there were no great surprises. The first box contained only a number of reports, files and the victim's handbag. The girl's clothing was missing. The bag contained very little except for a small amount of money in notes, a student card, some stamps and a letter. Nothing more.

Other items in the box included a watch, a few coins, a set of keys and a comb. Certainly there was nothing to assist the detectives in finding the young woman's killer. There was no jacket.

The contents of the second box were a variety of articles accumulated by the investigating team at the time. These consisted of items such as photographs, maps and drawings.

How much help these items would be, to the case, was easy to determine. A good fat zero would be an accurate assessment. This did not disappoint Harry. He had expected nothing. He was a realist and knew that some devastating evidence was not going to jump out of the boxes. It was going to take a lot to solve this case if it could be solved at all.

3

In the previous few months Harry and Emer's relationship had developed steadily. Neither were jumping headlong into the fray. They saw each other at work everyday and a great part of their weekends were spent together. But they maintained separate lives. Each had a family to worry about.

Sinead, Harry's oldest, had just married. However his other two daughters still lived at home. Fiona, Harry's second child, was pregnant. The father was not in the picture and Harry worried about her. The youngest, Rita, was at college. Her life consisted of a mix of study and socialising.

Emer had her worries as well. The revelation that her son, Brian, was gay had come like a bolt out of the blue. It had never crossed her mind that that this might be his orientation. Outwardly she had not displayed any anxiety or negativity. Brian would have judged her response to his revelation as being positive.

It was strange, she had observed, how different generations saw situations. Her daughter, a garda recruit, had accepted her brother's relationship unreservedly. And as Harry had once remarked, Nuala had accepted both her mother's and her brother's new love lives with equal enthusiasm.

The next morning the squad all gathered early. The work on the previous case had been completed and they were ready for fresh pastures.

'It must be obvious to us all,' Harry began, 'that it will take a minor miracle to solve this case. Joyce wants us to give it a shot but this is not an open ended assignment. He will review any progress in a fortnight and will decide whether we are to continue with the case. If we make some headway we'll continue, if not it will be over.'

Harry paused for a moment to gauge the reaction.

'If the chances of a charge are remote, why reopen the case at all?' Pete Halpin asked.

'I suppose there are two answers to that. First of all, Joyce and myself have a personal interest. We were both young gardaí, stationed in Bray, when the killing took place. We were the first gardaí on the scene. It was our first murder. Neither of us were involved in the subsequent investigation but the lack of a conviction has irked us ever since. The second reason is, of course, that new information has come to light so we have a responsibility to take it on board.'

Halpin was satisfied, but Dan McCarthy wanted to know more.

'Harry, why is the name of the alleged perpetrator blacked out on the copies of the letter we received?'

It was Billy Lynch who answered.

'Dan, there is only one possible reason and that is, that the name is dynamite and the avoidance of mistakes and snooping eyes from outside this room must be prevented for the moment.'

Harry nodded his agreement then added, 'for the present, it's best kept confidential. There is nothing to sustain the assertion so for the time being I'm keeping it to myself.'

It was then on to the case.

'There are several preliminary tasks that we need to do first. Emer, I want you to go through the files. Organise them and see what they can tell us if anything. Pete, you go through the boxes and prepare an inventory of what is there and then you can give Emer a hand.'

Harry paused for a moment before continuing.

'Newspaper reports Dan, I want you to go through old issues of the papers and see what was reported. There probably wasn't much but you never know. Start with the Bray People. It is a weekly and I need copies of all the issues for the weeks before and after the murder. I don't need originals, photocopies will do.'

Harry wasn't going to give any of the routine chores to Billy. He wasn't any good at them and besides he had something special for his old friend.

'Billy, I want you to find me the guy who wrote the letter.'

This was just the kind of assignment that Billy Lynch revelled in. Digging for hidden information and doing it alone. He was good at this, in fact nobody did it better.

Over his years in the force Harry had noticed that there was a common feature that marked all good police men and women. This was the belief that every victim was entitled to justice. It was not so much the punishment meted out to the perpetrator but the fact that he had to answer for his actions. With the case in hand, although it was less than a day old, he could sense from his team the belief that justice had been delayed for Joanne Boylan, for far too long.

Harry left them to their assignments. The bright autumn day attracted him for his walk. He had become reasonably diligent with regard to his exercise. It was just over six months since his bypass operation. He had recovered well, but he knew he was still not back to his old self. Maybe he never would be, but he was good enough for the life he led.

Billy Lynch had left the station within minutes of receiving his assignment. He was pleased with what he had been given. He enjoyed working with Harry Tinto. He had done well, for Harry, in the Cooper case back in June. It looked like he was going to be with Harry until his retirement.

When Jack Doyle had brought him in to work for him, it had been a gift and then when Doyle had been moved on to the clerical killings and Harry had replaced him it had been his birthday and Christmas all rolled up into one. And now months later, with Doyle retired for health reasons, he was still at Harry's side and it was beginning to look to him like there had been some collusion on Doyle's and Tinto's part to keep him out of trouble and safe until he retired. The thought moved him deeply.

His first thoughts of his assignment led him to the conclusion that if his prey was dead, then it would be much simpler to locate him. If alive, it would be nearly impossible. He would presume, for the present, that the man had died.

Suicide always necessitated a post mortem and therefore records would be available. There would be a considerable number of post mortems performed in the city over a period of days but the information he had at his disposal could eliminate many of them from his inquiry.

The individual in question was male, in his mid fifties. He was suffering from terminal cancer. The age was just a calculated guess, if he was a student in seventy seven then mid fifties fitted. It was a matter of checking with the coroner's office to begin with. The remains of a suicide would not be taken to a hospital but to the City Morgue. This, of course, presumed that the man had died in the capital. There was nothing to support that presumption.

However, Billy was in luck. There had indeed been a suicide matching the specifications given. The body of a man had been recovered from the sea in Dun Laoghaire the previous day. It was calculated that he had been in the water for twenty four hours. It would seem likely that he had posted his letter to Donal Joyce and had died on the same day.

The name Martin Devereaux meant nothing to Billy and the information that the coroner's office was able to give him did not help a lot. Devereaux had indeed been suffering from cancer and it was terminal. He had died from drowning. A routine suicide was the pathologist's conclusion.

The deceased had an address in Cabinteely. The remains had been released already and taken to a funeral home in Blackrock. The coroner's office didn't know when the removal was to take place. Billy knew that the Irish Independent would answer that question for him.

Harry was familiar with the name Martin Devereaux. Although he had never met the man, he knew that Devereaux was involved in academia. Sinead, his eldest, had taken some of his courses at university and from what she had said, Harry knew, that he was a man respected by both his peers and his students. Harry found it almost unbelievable that such a man might, even in the wildness of youth, have been involved in the death of another.

Billy had been very quick with the identification and had brought up the question of the man's removal. A quick check of The Irish Independent had shown that the remains were being taken to the church that evening.

Harry would go along and observe. Maybe, a certain government minister might attend to pay his last respects.

Emer had literally got the dirty job. The files were filthy with thirty years of accumulated dust but she endeavoured not to worry about her clothes.

The modus operandi that she operated was first to separate the documents into three categories. The first category was for the reports filed by the investigators at the time. The second grouping would contain all the technical reports and the final classification would be all the statements taken in the case.

By lunchtime she had completed that part of her task. Time was needed to clean herself up a bit but the dust was everywhere, in her hair, on her face, on her hands. She felt grubby and knew that only a shower would rectify the situation but that would have to wait until later.

During the afternoon the focus would be on reading the aged paperwork. She began with the police reports. Practically all of them were written in longhand.

Most of the reports were the work of the officer in charge of investigation, a man called John O'Leary. Emer noted the name. Harry would want to know if the man was still alive. If he was, he might remember something useful.

The reports were particularly skimpy. To Emer's eyes, they were long on the investigative effort and short on evidence and clues as to who might have perpetrated the ghastly deed. She could feel the frustration of the writer when there was so little progress to report. The perpetrator had left nothing to follow up.

Neither had a motive for the killing been identified. Joanne Boylan had led an exemplary life. There were no dark sides to her existence. She was hard working and serious, pretty and bright. There were no relatives but she had plenty of friends, whose reaction to her killing had been disbelief. Who would have wanted to terminate her life? Nobody could tell. Nobody could suggest a reason for the killing.

It was in one of O'Leary's last reports that he discussed the possibility of Joanne's death being a random killing. A murder carried out without a motive. This suggested that the killing was motivated by evil or insanity. Ultimately, O'Leary dismissed his thesis. That kind of thing, in his experience, did not happen in Ireland. It was the stuff of American crime novels and films.

The original team had worked long and hard on the case with nothing to show for their efforts. After four weeks the investigation was scaled down and a fortnight later, it was discontinued.

'Until now,' Emer thought.

The case had the look of a dead end to her but what did she know about murder? This was only the third case she had participated in. But the sadness that she felt for Joanne Boylan was real and she wished that the student, who had died so young all those years ago, could rest in peace.

Pete Halpin had found nothing of any value in the boxes. So after lunch he set about reading through the technical reports. He started with the post mortem.

Joanne Boylan had been in perfect health the night she died. The pathologist had calculated that she had died in the early hours of the morning, roughly eight hours before her body was discovered. Death had been caused by a series of stab wounds to the girl's chest. The spread of the wounds suggested that the killer had little knowledge of the vital points of the human anatomy. There was significant bruising to the girl's face and mouth which indicated that the killer had grabbed her face with his hand. It was a safe assumption that Joanne Boylan had been attacked from behind. She had never seen her killer.

Furthermore, there were other conclusions that could be drawn. The victim was a taller than the average girl at five foot seven inches, therefore her assailant would have been considerably taller, certainly six foot and maybe more. He would have been strong as well.

Pete stopped for some time. He located a street map of Bray and, with the help of some Bluetack, he affixed it to a wall in the incident room. The hotel where Joanne had worked was at the northern end of the mile long promenade and Pete, who knew the geography of the town well, marked the map with an H in a spot which approximated with the International Hotel.

Joanne had lived in a small bungalow on Sidmonton Road. This was a long street which ran parallel to the Strand Road and the promenade. The house couldn't have been far from where the girl had worked.

Pete was unsure of exactly where the bungalow was, so he made no mark on his map. It would be time enough when he knew for certain. The reports by the Technical Bureau provided a great deal of information relating to the location where the girl was found. But even at the time, it had proved to be of little assistance. It would certainly prove to be of no help now. Pete knew that if they had the jacket, referred to in the letter, matters might be different however, it hadn't been located, so there was little point in speculating.

'How did we all do?' Harry asked when he convened a meeting at three thirty.

'Emer, seeing you had the dusty job, you can start.'

Emer began by summarising what she had done in the morning, then she moved on to what she had gleaned from the reports she had read. She told her colleagues that, to her inexperienced eyes, she had found nothing constructive. The only thing that struck her was John O'Leary's speculation that the victim might have been selected at random. She had inquired about O'Leary but had been told that he had died years ago.

Harry immediately took her up on the issue of random selection and asked her to give a detailed rundown on the old policeman's theory.

'O'Leary summed it up,' she said 'if there is no motive then there is no link between the killer and his victim and that limits enormously the paths that an investigation can travel.'

Harry nodded.

'That could be it,' he said. 'Did the reports indicate whether that line of inquiry was ever examined?'

'No, the idea was dismissed as being absurd. O'Leary felt that unmotivated killings only happen in fiction,' she replied.

The others had little to report. Billy's success in identifying Donal Joyce's correspondent was already known to all the team. Pete had nothing positive to report and Dan had drawn an apparent blank with the newspapers.

'Did you get the issue of the Bray People published the week prior to the killing?' Pete asked.

'Yes, I have it here,' Dan replied 'but it is of little use. You can have a look yourself.' And he handed the photocopies over to his colleague.

They continued to discuss the various aspects of the case for another fifteen minutes and then Harry broke up the meeting.

St. Bridget's Church, in Cabinteely, is small and can seat only a few hundred souls at most. Martin Devereaux's remains were due to arrive there at five thirty. Harry Tinto was there a little after five.

He was not there to pay his respects to the deceased but rather to observe those who did. He was interested in one person alone. He was anxious to see whether Devereaux's old school friend, Dennis Hogan, would make an appearance.

Harry stood by the wall on the opposite side of the road from the church. From there he could view all who came to pay their respects. By five fifteen a large crowd had gathered, some had gone inside while most, as is the custom in some parts of Ireland, stayed outside to await the arrival of the remains.

At five twenty five a dark Mercedes pulled in a short distance from the church door and from it Dennis Hogan alighted.

The detective stayed where he was. The objective of his attendance at the removal had been achieved. However he was surprised at how large a man Hogan was, certainly over six foot. He looked trim and fit for a man in his middle years and Harry remembered the pathology report that Pete had shown him earlier. The killer was of strong build and over six foot tall.

'It could be,' Harry thought.

4

Emer was just out of the shower when Harry phoned. The dust of the day was now relegated to the history books. She was feeling good and was glad of the phone call.

It was a grand autumn evening and the drive to Wicklow was very pleasant. A drink and a bite to eat in the pleasant little village of Laragh was what was on offer. It was the perfect antidote to a hard day at the station.

Harry introduced the topic of their new case as they bypassed Bray.

'This is going to be very hard to pull off,' he confided, 'I doubt if we will ever get a conviction unless there is some kind of miracle and I'm afraid that the humble garda is never on the receiving end of such munificence.'

'My impression is that unless we get a confession from someone you will be right.' Emer said.

'You know what I would be satisfied with? Even if we had no evidence to prove it, simply to know with certainty who killed the girl. Then we could let him know, that his murder was less than perfect and that even after all this time we were still interested. At least, he might have some sleepless nights.'

There was a brief silence as they both thought about what Harry had just said.

'You know,' Emer said as she broke the silence, 'if what O'Leary wrote was true, our man would be a vicious individual, a psychopath. A person unable to distinguish right from wrong and confident in his own capability to survive anything, come what may. You know Harry, if he got away with it once, he may have tried again.'

Harry stared at her.

'Emer, that thought never crossed my mind. But someone, who believes he has committed the perfect crime, might have the arrogance to want to do it all over again. You know, he may have repeated it a number of times.'

Harry said nothing for a few seconds.

'Emer, I think what you said needs looking into but the thought of more senseless, motiveless killings of innocent people is a horror story.'

Their evening in Laragh was pleasant and enjoyable. They spoke no more of their work. They both had families and the comings and goings of their young people provided ample scope for conversation.

As they drove back Harry said.

'I have a confession to make.'

Emer had no idea what to expect.

'Before this case came up,' he continued 'I was going to ask if you would come away with me for a short break?'

'If you're asking me now, the answer is yes,' Emer replied.

'So how about going to New York for five or six days at the end of October?'

'It's a long time since I was there. New York would be great.'

They chatted easily for the rest of the journey home, both knowing that their relationship was now heading for a new and different plateau. Emer always knew it would get there someday but Harry had baggage and it had taken him longer to reach this point of commitment.

That evening Pete had taken a drive to County Wicklow as well but he had turned off into Bray. He had the address of Joanne Boylan's house. He had no difficulty locating the address. It was at the town end of Sidmonton Road, just a short distance from the International Hotel.

He had wondered earlier about the discos that might have operated in Bray in the late seventies. There would be court records of licenses granted but it would be a mighty job to locate them after thirty years and that would not tell them which establishments were open on the night of the killing. Dan McCarthy had given him the solution when he had given him the copies of the Bray People.

Local papers were heavy with local news, local social events and local sports. They were also loaded with local advertising. Entertainment events advertised heavily. The paper would certainly carry an advertisement for any weekend disco that might be on.

As he sat in his car, close to the promenade, he was not interested in the pleasant view of the sea, Bray Head to the south and Killiney towards the north. He was scouring McCarthy's papers for advertisements for discos. He had found only one. It was called Saracens. It had been open on the night of the killing. They had advertised the appearance of a well known radio disc jockey called Fab Vinny. Pete remembered him.

'Tempus fugit,' he thought.

The paper gave no indication of where Saracens had been located. The bulk of local police would probably be too young to have heard of the place and the older ones would almost certainly have been stationed elsewhere at the time. Besides, discos had a habit of changing name and location frequently.

Pete knew how he would find the location of Saracens. It would be easy he thought and it was. Leaving his car, he walked across the green open space to the promenade and sat down on a wooden seat. There were plenty of people enjoying a leisurely autumn evening stroll. All Pete had to do was to wait for the right people. He hadn't long to wait.

In the distance he saw a likely target, a couple probably in their mid to late fifties. If they were from Bray, it was almost certain that they would have known the discos of thirty years ago.

As they approached, Pete stood up and introduced himself by presenting his identification.

'I would be obliged if you could help me,' he began.

'Could I ask if either of you are from Bray?'

Pete was in luck. They were both from the town and had lived there all their lives.

'I'm looking for the location of the old Saracens disco,' he explained, 'it was popular, I believe, about thirty years ago.'

'That place is long gone, but I know where it was,' the man told Pete.

'It was on the Strand Road just up from the railway station. It's Claude's Amusement Arcade now.'

Pete thanked them for their assistance and with his mission now completed, he would have a pint before going home. He was feeling quite satisfied with himself.

Emer's comment on the possibility of the killer having struck, on more than one occasion, remained with Harry. Motiveless, violent crimes were rare. Harry figured that if there is no reason for the act then the objective must be the experience of the kill. He reasoned that if the killer felt pleasure or fulfilment from the act, then he might want to repeat the experience. The more he thought about it the more Harry feared that it could be possible.

Harry announced to his small team his decision to extend the investigation.

'The joker who did this,' he told them, 'may have tried a second time. I know it is only a hunch but there is some logic to it. He would be smart enough not to try Bray again but anywhere would do. The victim is selected at random so any street of any town would do. He would have no preferences.'

'Would the circumstances be the same?' Pete asked.

'I think so, but not in every detail. He would aspire to replicate the previous killing, to relive the pleasure of the kill. I think the victim will always be a woman. She would be attacked from the rear and sent to her God by the blade of a knife. If he is the tall large man that I'm told he is, there would be no sense in him taking on someone whose resistance might prove a problem for him.'

'Emer, I want you to contact every division in the country. Find out if there are any unsolved murder cases involving a female victim apparently with no motive for the killing, where a knife was the murder weapon. We want them to go back the full thirty years. Go directly to the Chief Superintendent in each area and tell them it's for me.'

Harry arrived at Donal Joyce's office without an appointment but was sent in straight away.

'That was quick work Harry. Have you tied it all up in a day?'

They both laughed.

'Seriously, I think there could be others.' Harry began.

'Others, you mean killings?'

26

'Yes, I think there is some chance that this guy, Hogan or whoever it is, has killed more than once.'

'That's a quick conclusion to come to. Is there any evidence to back it up?' Joyce asked.

'No evidence, just logic.'

Harry outlined to his superior officer his reasoning. There is always a motive he explained but it could be as mindless as just wanting to derive pleasure from a kill. If the incident in Bray satisfied him then he might want to kill again and as morality was clearly not an issue for him, there was nothing to stop another killing.

Joyce could see clearly where Harry's thinking was coming from and he could find no flaws in his deductions.

'What do you propose to do with this?' he asked.

'I've started searching for unsolved killings which have similarities to this one. All young women, all stabbed, with no motive and probably no witnesses or suspects.'

'Keep at it Harry, if we have a maniac out there, he needs to be found. For all we know more deaths could be on the way. Is there anything else?'

'Yes, there is. The Taoiseach, Matt Dolan, I need to see him.'

Joyce knew that Harry Tinto was not asking for permission, he was just informing a superior officer of his intentions.

'Yes, the Taoiseach should be briefed about Hogan,' Joyce answered.

When Harry got back, he called Billy Lynch to the inner office. He had something special for him.

'What I tell you, Billy, doesn't leave this room. I'll tell the others later.'

Harry didn't need to wait for a reply. He knew Lynch too well.

'Dennis Hogan, the minister, is the man named in the Devereaux statement.'

'God, Harry, that's a mess.' Billy replied.

'I want you to prepare a profile of this character. I'm not interested in what he promised and what he delivered, what he said or what he supported. I'm interested in where he was, where he lived and where he spoke. Later we may be able to reduce the parameters of your research but not for now. Remember Billy, no notes lying around, this is just between you and me.'

It was another plus in working for Harry Tinto. This was an important job and Billy appreciated the trust in being told what only Joyce and Harry knew. Of course, Harry didn't need to mention the notes. He would have known that Billy never wrote anything down apart from the final report.

'Where the hell will I start?' Billy asked himself as he left the building. He needed to think, to work out a strategy to follow, in his quest to deliver to Harry Tinto exactly what the superintendent needed. It would not be easy. As Billy Lynch walked towards Westmoreland Street, he was unaware that he was humming.

There are twenty six divisions in the Garda Síochána and Emer had been in contact with most of them. She was amazed at the influence that the name Tinto had, in getting through to the men at the top.

Everyone listened to what she had to say and all promised to get back to her as soon as possible.

It was just after lunch when Emer contacted the Galway West division. The Chief Superintendent was away for a few days so she was speaking to his secretary, Mary Murphy.

'If you give me an outline of your query, I'll bring it to his attention when he gets back.'

Emer told her what she was looking for. Unsolved killings of young women, apparently without motive. The murder weapon was probably a knife. Anytime in the last thirty three years.

'You know, if you need this quickly, I'll give you a number. It's a Sergeant Michael Baker. He's well over seventy now but had been stationed in the Galway area throughout his career. He's in good health and has a sound mind, with a memory like an elephant. If anything, like what you have described, happened on his watch, he will remember it.'

Emer thanked Mary and then rang Michael Baker.

She struck gold.

Matt Dolan was very surprised when he was told that a Harry Tinto had contacted his office. Dolan noted that Tinto had not said who he was or what he wanted.

Matt Dolan was the Taoiseach, and both his and Harry Tinto's paths had crossed earlier in the year. Dolan had made the error of underestimating the policeman. It was a mistake he would not repeat. Matt Dolan took the number Harry had given and phoned the detective himself.

Later that afternoon Harry gathered Emer, Dan and Pete and told them who their suspect was. He had realised that they could not work effectively in the dark and the lack of information might result in something being passed over. Anyway not telling them suggested a lack of trust and that was not Tinto's way of doing things.

Billy Lynch's first call had been to the party's central office and his first stop had been to The Irish Times. Where better to get a potted biography of Dennis Hogan than from a newspaper published on the day after his appointment to the cabinet. The party office had provided the date when the promotion had occurred.

Hogan had been appointed Minister for Defence and Billy learned from The Irish Times that Hogan's promotion had been well received as well as having been widely predicted. He had served a long apprenticeship in the parliamentary party. He had for years been seen as possible leadership material.

But Billy knew that in the medium term that was not to be. A leadership contest five years ago had selected Matt Dolan for the number one job.

Delving further into back issues revealed that Hogan had made a steady but not spectacular assent up the ministerial ladder to the senior ministry he now occupied.

Emer's conversation with Sergeant Baker was revealing. There had been a killing in Galway and he remembered it well. A young woman had been found dead, murdered on the promenade in Salthill very early one morning. He had been the sergeant in the local station at the time. It would be twelve years ago last April twenty first. Michael Baker expressed a strong willingness to be of assistance in whatever way he could.

'I still get annoyed, even after all this time, when I think of that girl.' He concluded.

The afternoon meeting started sometime after four. And Harry let them all have their say. Emer outlined what she had done during the day. Although most divisions had promised to report back later in the day nothing had materialized so far. At the conclusion she told of her conversation with Michael Baker.

'Ok,' Harry announced, 'Dan and I are going to Galway in the morning. We'll take the early train. Emer, set up an appointment to meet Baker and get the Galway station to have a car to meet us. Dan, you'll go to the local paper, it's the Connaught Tribune and get a copy of the paper for the week following April 21st 1999. Come to think of it Dan, I think there is another local paper, you may need to check that out. We will both meet Michael Baker first. If he is the kind of cop I think he is, we might be in luck.'

Emer was to continue with her quest to find unsolved murders that fitted the pattern while Billy would carry on with his assignment.

Harry was disturbed to think that there might be another girl who had died in similar circumstances and by the same hand. And if that proved to be the case and the length of time between killings was taken into account, there was the possibility that there could be several more deaths that were still to be uncovered.

Then there was their suspect, Dennis Hogan, a man of power and wealth, celebrity and influence and now he, Harry Tinto, was about to bring him down even though no guilt had yet been established.

Matt Dolan had called and arranged to meet Harry in the bar of the Burlington Hotel at seven that evening. It was a kind of déjà vu. It was the same arrangement as last time. The only difference being that Emer was with him on the previous occasion.

The Taoiseach was on time and on this occasion arrived without an entourage. He walked directly to Harry.

'Well Harry, I didn't expect to see you again so soon,' the politician said. 'Is it business or personal?'

'It's unofficial, Taoiseach but there is something I believe you should be aware of.'

The conversation ceased for a few moments, when a waiter came to them to take their order. Both would have coffee.

'Two days ago,' Harry continued, 'I began an investigation into the death of a young woman who was killed more than thirty years ago. It's what is termed nowadays as a cold case. All this came about as the result of an unsigned letter from an unidentified man. He wrote that he intended to end his life and he wanted to clear up the one remaining unresolved issue in his life. He admitted to being an accessory to the crime along with several others.'

The waiter arrived and Harry paused. When the coffees were before them, Harry continued.

'A murder that couldn't be solved three decades ago would have no chance of success now unless there was something new and significant. The letter did provide new information. It identified the killer. Our informant named one of your ministers as the killer.'

Matt Dolan was speechless.

'I will tell you who it is if you wish, however you might prefer not to know his identity at this time. It's up to you.'

'A killer in my administration, a murderer at the Cabinet table. It's unbelievable. Yes, tell me more and tell me who.'

Harry had brought with him a copy of the confession and handed it to the Taoiseach. Matt Dolan read it a couple of times before handing it back.

'Dennis Hogan and I are more rivals than colleagues. We're certainly not friends but I wouldn't have thought he was capable of murder.'

Taking the letter back, the Taoiseach read it again.

'This is unbelievable,' was all he could say.

Harry explained to him that at this point there was no evidence whatsoever to link Hogan to the killing. However, the investigation had identified the writer, a man called Martin Devereaux.

'I know Martin Devereaux, at least I did. He died just the other day.'

Dolan stopped, the penny had dropped. Devereaux had had terminal cancer and he had taken his own life. Devereaux and Hogan knew one another. They went to school together but they were not close friends.

Harry broke into Matt Dolan's thoughts.

'Taoiseach, we have only a very slim chance of making a charge in the case and much less of getting a conviction. What we are doing is proceeding with the investigation on the basis that the death of Joanne Boylan was not a once off incident. There was no motive for the killing, at least no known reason, so the killing must have satisfied a psychological need. If that was the case then it is probable that there were other killings.'

Harry Tinto was finished but Dolan said nothing for a while. Then calling over the waiter he ordered more coffee. He was not finished. Harry knew that the Taoiseach's thoughts at that moment were political.

Finally he asked.

'Harry, how many people know about this?' he asked

'Very few, my small team, that's four, Donal Joyce, yourself and myself. That's all, a total of seven.'

'Thanks Harry, I appreciate you telling me.'

Harry could sense that Dolan was reluctant to go. He had something else on his mind and it had nothing to do with the present situation.

'The little girl,' he eventually asked 'how is she?'

Earlier in the year, on another case, Harry had discovered that Dolan, unknown to himself, had an eleven year old daughter who had been adopted. The little girl was safe and secure, loved and cherished in her adoptive family and wanted for nothing. At the time Harry saw pain in Matt Dolan, a sense of loss for something he had not known. He could still see it in his face.

'You know Taoiseach, I was going to contact you before this business cropped up. I had a phone call last week from her family and they asked me to pass on a message to you. Her name is Aishling, she is a joy. When she asks they will tell her everything and if she is ever in any need they will certainly come to you.'

Matt Dolan just nodded

Then taking an envelope from his pocket, Harry handed it to the Taoiseach. It was unsealed. Inside were three very recent photographs of a beautiful eleven year old. Dolan took them out carefully and looked at them for a long time.

'Just like her mother, just like Theresa.' was all he said.

5

Billy had put together the bones of a biography of Dennis Hogan. He had been born in 1956 in Ballinasloe. His father had been a civil servant. When Hogan was about six years old, a transfer with promotion, moved the family to the east coast and they settled in the resort town of Greystones.

His initial schooling was in Greystones but his secondary education took place in St. Dominick's College in Dublin. It was then, and still is today, a well regarded educational establishment for boys. He remained there for six years before moving on to university in 1974 to study Arts.

A bright student, the burdens of getting a degree were not a heavy load for him. He involved himself in college activities with a vengeance and showed particular ability at debating. He discovered politics and took to it like a duck to water.

It seemed as if he had been born lucky. Success was for him the norm. Others appeared to have to earn it but it had always been handed to him on a plate. Then something changed. He failed his final exams. Failure, a word he had never contemplated, was now embedded in his being. He never returned to finish the degree.

Through contacts, from his school days in St. Dominick's, he got employment with a prominent auctioneering firm and he prospered.

Though now out of the academic environment of the university, he maintained his interest in politics and transferred his party membership to a cumann in South Dublin.

By 1980 he was married and the first opportunity to present himself for public office materialised and he won a seat easily on Dublin County Council.

He worked hard for the party and his constituents. He came to be seen as someone destined to do well on the national stage. Hogan was selected to contest the parliamentary elections in 1982 and although the party he represented fared well at the polls, he was not elected.

A few years later, when the party was re-elected, he had been elected easily. He was thirty five years old.

During the succeeding years, Hogan was elevated to the cabinet. Different administrations saw him climb the cabinet ladder. Eventually his ambitions became obvious and his luck ran out. He was dropped from ministerial office. He consolidated his support while out of favour and when the leadership became available he went for the top job. His opponent for the leadership was Matt Dolan. Hogan was defeated but Dolan had included him in his first cabinet and he remained there.

After he had left Matt Dolan, Harry phoned Emer, he wanted to meet her for a drink, but there was no reply. It was then that he remembered that she was meeting a friend for dinner so he rang his eldest daughter. Sinead had only been married a few months. It was her husband Martin who answered the phone. Yes, they would be delighted to meet him for a drink. Martin would drop Sinead off at Bakers in thirty minutes. He had a small errand to run but would be back in less than an hour.

Harry was seated when Sinead came in. She was the kind of girl who stood out in a crowd. She was 'tall and svelte and young and beautiful', just like the girl in the song. Stunning was the best word to describe her and Harry knew that it was from her mother that she had inherited that quality.

Harry was tired after the day but seeing Sinead come waltzing towards him made the weariness slip away. He wanted to ask her about Fiona, his second daughter. Harry wanted to know what he was not being told.

Although Fiona was living with him and he saw her every day, he didn't really know how she was. He would ask her and her answer was always the same. She was grand, that there were no problems, that it was a normal pregnancy. Maybe it was just parental anxiety but he didn't quite believe her. Rita, his youngest, was very attentive to Fiona and it was this that had triggered off his suspicions. He was a detective and unusual behaviour was always a signpost of something not being quite right. But Rita wasn't talking.

'Sinead,' Harry began after he had got her a drink, 'I know something is up with Fiona. I'm being kept in the dark. Fiona won't tell me and you know Rita, she won't tell me either.'

'Look Dad, Fiona just doesn't want to worry you. It's something you can't do anything about. She has some kind of a blood problem that is serious enough to require monitoring but not sufficient to require any kind of intervention. It will not harm Fiona, it will not damage the baby but there is a risk of a miscarriage. Let her be, Dad, if there is something you should know, I promise I will tell you.'

Harry knew he would have to be satisfied with that, he also knew that Sinead would be as good as her word.

'Now Dad, to change the subject, when is the big day? When are you and Emer going to tie the knot?'

She had certainly changed the subject and had put him on the back foot. He knew it and she knew it but she didn't push the issue. In the distance they saw Martin coming their way.

When he got home there was a message on the machine from Emer. She was sorry they had missed each other and she told him to enjoy his trip to Galway.

Michael Baker answered the door and led his two colleagues into his sitting room. Baker was a tall man even for a Garda. He was well over six foot. He was slim and straight, some achievement for a man of his years. He offered coffee which was accepted and he left the room to get the refreshments. It took him only a minute and Harry knew that the preparations had been made well in advance.

They chatted easily while they enjoyed the coffee. It was Michael Baker who introduced the issue.

'The young woman I spoke to yesterday said you are interested in the Sarah Malone case,' he said.

'Yes,' Harry answered, 'we're investigating a killing that occurred thirty years ago that has never been solved. The victim was a young woman, about twenty. There was no apparent motive and she was killed with a knife. We think that she might have been selected at random and we think that there may have been other similar killings over the years.'

Michael Baker lit his pipe and leaned back on his chair.

'Sarah Malone was found in the shelter at the top of the promenade near Threadneedle Road. I was the first garda on the scene. She was just lying there, a bundle on the concrete floor. There was blood all over the place. Her clothes were not disturbed. The post mortem confirmed that she had not been sexually molested and as in your own case, the weapon used was a knife.'

Baker stopped for a few moments to relight his pipe before continuing.

'She was only nineteen years old and a university student. A lot of effort went into the investigation but we got nowhere. We never progressed, even to the stage where we had identified a suspect. The murder squad kept at it for months then it just petered out. The case was never re-activated, there was no reason to, at least until now.'

Harry asked Michael Baker, in so far as he could, to relate what the investigating team had done twelve years ago. Sergeant Baker obliged and Harry could find no fault with their work.

Harry was on the return Dublin train by three o'clock. He would be at Heuston Station at six. Harry had left Dan in Galway and apart from getting the back issues of the local papers, he was to examine all the files on the case and to bring back with him whatever he could on the Sarah Malone killing.

Back in Dublin, events were moving ahead and Emer and Pete were under pressure. Most divisions were reporting back and most had nothing to report. The exceptions were Cork and Limerick. Both cities had killings that fitted the specifications exactly. Young women knifed to death without any apparent motive. However a very long period of time had elapsed between killings. The girl from Cork had died in the early 80's, the Limerick victim was murdered just five years ago.

Emer had had an idea and had made an urgent request to Cork to fax up the post mortem report. She got Dan to do the same in Galway. Pete was going to contact Henry Street and get the Limerick post mortem. She had contacted Harry on his mobile and he was more than pleased with her initiative.

It was imperative to determine whether the common features of the four killings were just a series of coincidences or the mark of a

36

single killer. As he thought about the interview with the proud old cop, a fourth common factor occurred to him. All the killings took place in university towns. Galway, Cork and Limerick were certainly such places. Bray was a stretch but the university was only ten miles away.

Emer's call got him thinking in a different direction. He called her back to get the others to find out whether the people who carried out the post mortems were still alive and available. The probability was that they were, with the possible exception of Bray.

After he left Harry, Dan visited the Tribune's offices in Galway and found them most helpful. It would take just half an hour to produce a hard copy for him. They also told him to try The Advertiser, the other local paper, which he did.

By six o'clock the files on the Sarah Malone case had not been gathered together. Garda storage was not as accessible or as modern as the newspapers, but the local men would have assembled everything by nine the next morning.

Dan was not put out by the prospect of a stay in Galway, particularly as it was at the taxpayer's expense. A few of the local fellows had suggested a night out on the town for their illustrious colleague. There was nothing for him to do but to enjoy the pleasures of the western tourist capital, good drink, good food and bad women.

'Well,' he thought, 'two out three wouldn't be bad'.

If Hogan was a suspect, one strand needed urgent investigation. Had the minister the opportunity to kill the girls? If it materialised that he hadn't the opportunity, then the case would fall.

Those were Billy's thoughts. He wondered what Hogan would say about his movements on the night or nights in question.

Nobody could possibly be expected to be able to remember where they might have been on a specific night thirty three years ago. It was asking the impossible and if someone had the answer, it certainly raised a question mark.

Billy did a little arithmetic. In 1977 Dennis Hogan was twenty one years old and had just completed three years at university. He had left college with nothing to show for his efforts or lack of efforts, as was probably the case.

Where was he on the night in question? The exams were over, the results were out. He had not yet started his job in the auctioneering firm. He could have been anywhere. He could, as many did in those times, have gone to the UK or New York to work for the summer. Maybe he was deciding on his future. Maybe he was at home in Greystones.

Billy knew how he would approach the situation. Hogan's old friends from St. Dominick's College and university would unwittingly fill in the gaps. He would start with the secondary school.

Lynch knew that prestigious schools had several aspects to them that could assist him. St. Dominick's would certainly have a Past Pupils' Union which would enable him to trace many of the school's old boys. Then there was the probability that the school published a yearbook. Annuals usually contained class photographs and the names of all the students. The school's archives would have copies.

Harry got the team together early the next morning. They were all there except for Dan. Emer had all four post mortem reports and had given a copy of each, to everyone. To their unqualified minds it seemed that the reports were very alike but Harry wanted more.

'Emer,' he said, 'I think you said that the pathologist who carried out the Limerick post mortem is available.'

Emer nodded.

'I want you to see him. Bring all four reports with you and ask for any differences and similarities that he might note. The big question to be put to him is whether all four killings could be the work of the same person.'

'He's now working in Wexford, Harry.'

'Then enjoy your day trip to the sunny South East,' he said.

'Billy, I want you to continue with what you are doing. I think your approach is correct. Pete, I need you to hold the fort here for the day. Keep in touch with us all and if Dan gets back early I want you both to scour each line of the Galway newspapers for any reference to a meeting or event that one might expect the presence of a national politician.'

Before his surgery, earlier in the year, Harry had never taken much exercise, now, on his physician's advice, walking was a serious part of his daily regime. He found it difficult, at first, to make time for it, particularly after his return to work. However, it was no longer a chore, just an enjoyable part of the day. Some of the pleasure came from being alone and undisturbed, which gave him time to think and time to plan.

As he strolled on the promenade in Clontarf, he felt a certainty that all the girls had been killed by the same person and that perpetrator was Hogan. He recognised that the mind of this rogue male was beyond his understanding. It was beyond him why someone would kill another person without reason. He could see and understand a killing brought on by passion or greed or self preservation. But this, no!

Harry needed someone to guide him, someone who understood the workings of the human mind even at its most deviant. He wasn't sure whether it was a psychologist or psychiatrist that was required. Television programmes had a name for the person he needed. They called them profilers.

Emer had enjoyed the drive to Wexford. It could not have been more than eighty miles and there was plenty of sunshine and little traffic. She thought of her children and her growing acceptance of her son's orientation. What had surprised her most was how his father had accepted Brian's orientation so easily. For him it wasn't an issue, but it was not the same for him. He had a second family, a boy and girl.

And then there was Harry. She knew that she wanted to be with him, that she loved him and that he loved her. There were no obstacles. Both their families had no reservations about their parents' new relationship. However Harry was still in slow motion. What he needed was a bit of a push.

John Davitt, the pathologist, took his time reading all four reports. He started with his own. It was four years ago and in that time he had examined the remains of hundreds of people and he had no recollection of the case.

Emer left him to his quest and went for a coffee in the hospital cafeteria. It was an hour before Dr. Davitt joined her.

'Sergeant Ryan, as I understand it, you are endeavouring to establish whether all four victims were killed by the same person. My opinion, as a pathologist, is an overwhelming yes. I would bet a year's salary that you have four killings and one killer.'

Emer had tried to contact Harry but either his phone was turned off or he was out of range. She suspected it was the former. That meant he was walking and she was pleased.

How could one find out if Dennis Hogan had been in the locations where the killings took place. It had originally appeared an impossible task but Harry thought that he had found a way through it. He had asked Dan to get the local papers in Galway and Pete to get the papers in Limerick and Cork, for the weeks before and after the deaths. His intention was to search for information that would not be included in the records of the investigations.

Hogan was a politician and a high profile one at that. It was the nature of his lifestyle to be on the move, attending meetings, opening events, giving speeches and these occasions were fodder for the local press and were regularly given significant coverage, particularly if a well known personality was involved.

If Hogan had been in Galway and Limerick on the night of the murders, the provincial papers would have it. He rang Pete.

'Is Dan back yet?' He asked.

'Yes, he arrived back about twenty minutes ago. I'll pass you over.'

There was a brief lull while the young garda came to the phone.

'Dan, did you bring copies of the local newspapers with you?'

'Issues of both the Connaught Tribune and the Galway Advertiser published before and immediately after the killing.'

'What I want yourself and Pete to do is to go through both issues line by line and that includes the advertising. What you're looking for is any reference to any meeting, dinner, opening or anything that might involve a politician. You know who I'm talking about.'

Pete and Dan were deep into their task when Emer arrived back from Wexford. The two told her what they were doing and she offered to help them by making the coffee.

St. Dominick's College school annual was a very impressive affair and it provided Billy with what he needed, which was a list of all the students of class of 1974.

Armed with this list he contacted Don Kinsella. Kinsella was the current President of the Past Pupils' Union and Billy needed recent addresses and phone numbers for the names on his list. He knew that it might not be easy to extract those details from the union but he held an ace in his hand.

He was aware that institutions like St. Dominick's were very sensitive to any kind of public exposure and would do much to protect themselves from public scrutiny.

Billy's ace was that if the Union's co-operation was not forthcoming, a public request would be made to the boys of the class of '74 to contact the authorities to help them in their inquiries into ongoing criminal investigation.

This request if made, Billy knew would activate the newshounds and nothing good would come of it for the College. Don Kinsella would know this too.

Harry was preoccupied. The case had expanded significantly in the last twenty four hours. There were now four killings and if he were to go by John Davitt's interpretation of his own and the other post mortem reports there was only one perpetrator. Harry saw no reason to dispute the pathologist's judgement.

This had placed the detective in the horns of a dilemma. He needed additional resources to work with. There were four locations and they were spread across the country and with a team of five including himself it was simply too much. He knew that there would be little difficulty getting a greater allocation of personnel but there was a problem with their suspect. It would be vital that his identity remain confidential until such time as Harry decided that Hogan was to be taken in for questioning or an arrest was to be made or the man was to be charged. The more people involved in the investigation the greater the risk of a leak.

The next morning all five were gathered early.

'At the moment,' Harry began 'there are four murders and there are only five of us. With what we know or at least suspect, I doubt if there would be much difficulty getting extra resources but I've decided for the moment not to go down that road. There have been four deaths over thirty years that we are aware of, there may be more.'

Harry paused for a moment before continuing.

'So what do we know at this point. There appears to be no motive, just random slayings. All four victims were in their late teens or very early twenties, they were all girls. The four were university students and they were all slain with a knife. There clearly is no connection between the victims. The girl from Limerick hadn't been born at the time of Joanne Boylan's death. So where do we go from here?'

Harry paused for a few seconds.

'We'll concentrate on trying to establish whether Hogan had opportunity. We'll continue with our examination of the local papers in Galway, Limerick and Cork. Hogan wouldn't have had a public profile at the time of the Cork killing but look through those papers anyway.

Billy nodded. He had something to add to the pool of information and handed each of his colleagues the short biography of Hogan that he had assembled. In addition to the sketch of Hogan's earlier life his version included a summary of the ups and downs of the minister's political life.

It began with how Hogan, in the early eighties, had been elected to the Dublin County Council. He had done well enough to be selected as a Fianna Fail candidate for the election in eighty two. Although a councillor, he was still relatively unknown to the electorate and his great hopes were dashed with his failure to secure a seat. But like Lazarus, his fortune was reversed a few years later when another general election took place and he easily took his party's second seat. At this point he gave up the day job and became a highly motivated, ambitious full time TD.

His work and drive, his intelligence and political acumen soon saw him elevated to the status of minister for state. The middle 90's saw him in a full ministry. At this point the ultimate goal seemed within his reach and some elements in the media were beginning to speculate openly about his leadership ambitions.

A Cabinet reshuffle and Hogan's world collapsed, he was dropped. He took this very badly for a while but got his act together and after the election of '00, he was back in the cabinet.

So as the new millennium dawned his stock was high within the party and with the electorate. Incumbent Taoiseach Sean Doyle had indicated that he would not contest the next election and that he would step down within the year, allowing his successor sufficient time to get established. Dennis Hogan wanted to be that successor and many deputies supported his candidature. Even the bookies had installed him as the firm favourite.

The ballot in 2005 appeared to have been close but Matt Dolan got the job. Hogan didn't rant or sulk. It appears he took his defeat graciously and promised his full support and loyalty to the new leader and this appears to be what he had done.

Billy had done a good job in a short time and Harry acknowledged this.

A little later Harry was with Donal Joyce. The Chief Superintendent was sombre as he listened to Harry's summary of the facts, as he knew them to be.

'Four so far, Harry and you say there could be more to come.

'Unfortunately.'

'This Doctor Davitt is certain that the perpetrator is the same person in all four killings?' Joyce queried.

Harry nodded his agreement.

'What can I give you? What resources are needed?' Joyce asked.

'I need to talk to a profiler or a psychiatrist, I need to find out what makes this guy kill? What turns the killing on? Why the long gaps? Four murders over thirty years with gaps of ten, eight and seven years. There is no pattern to it that I can see.'

For a few minutes neither man said anything. It was like a case of, 'What next?'

As Harry returned to the incident room, he knew that it would be easy to get drawn into blind alleys. They needed to concentrate on their suspect and see whether a connection could be made. Only if opportunity could be established, then and only then could they move on. As far as Harry was concerned it didn't matter whether it was four or more murders and this was not callousness on his part. It was just that what was done was done and could not now be undone but the killer could strike again. This needed to be prevented.

With regard to the class of '74, Billy's plan was to establish who Hogan's friends were at school and which of these friendships survived into and through university. If he could determine who Hogan's friends were in university, it might be possible to discover who was with Devereaux and Hogan in the International Hotel on the night Joanne Boylan died.

Don Kinsella was an impressive man. His body language and accent, his size and confidence clearly stated that this was a man not to be trifled with. Billy had met such men before. They never intimidated him.

Billy outlined his needs. He wanted current addresses and phone numbers of the class of '74 or at least all of those the Union had

43

access to. He wanted to know who, if any, of the class were deceased. He needed all this quickly.

Billy could sense Kinsella's reluctance to get the Union and therefore the college involved, so the detective played his ace.

'Should the Union feel a reluctance to co-operate, which is its prerogative, it can refuse. However a refusal would require me to seek a court order to acquire that information. As I am dealing with a very serious crime I would get that order. Such an order would be very public, very newsworthy. It would give, I expect, the impression that the old boys of St. Dominick's College had something to hide. I'm sure the tabloids would have a field day.'

Billy was finished. His ace was the ace of trumps and Kinsella folded.

6

Donald Leyland was English and a psychiatrist. He had come to Dublin to do some research at Trinity College in 1995 and had stayed. He was now at the pinnacle of his profession and had been used by the Gardaí on several occasions, most recently by the detectives investigating the clerical killer murders.

Harry had never met Leyland but had no difficulty getting an appointment with him. The psychiatrist was always anxious to be of assistance to the Gardaí. He believed that the guardians of society's safety were entitled to assistance from the community when they needed it.

Harry outlined to Leyland the broad details of the case. The four deaths spread over three decades. Harry told Leyland that a pathologist had concluded that all four killings were perpetrated by the same person.

Leyland was told that there was a suspect. The individual had a long and successful career. Harry did not identify the suspect.

'What I hope to get from you, Doctor, is some idea of what might motivate this man to kill? What drives him? He has killed at least four times and I don't want someone else to die.'

'Would it be correct to infer that the individual you referred to, your suspect, is an aggressive and highly ambitious individual?'

'I have never met the man.' Harry answered. 'Certainly, I believe that he would be driven, as for aggression I would suspect it is an occupational necessity for him but, on this point, I could be wrong.'

Donald Leyland said nothing for a while and Harry allowed him the space to think.

'For a serial killer the long gaps between the acts of violence don't fit. It would seem to me that something triggers the killings. As the girls were random victims, there must be something in his life that acts as a trigger. And as these incidents, as far as you know, have occurred just four times over a very long period of time it must be the loss of something of enormous importance to him that starts him going. Marital squabbles, family problems, financial difficulties wouldn't seem to me to be the catalyst.'

Leyland was not finished but needed a little time.

'Would there be a passion in this man's life which totally consumes him?' the psychiatrist asked. 'And I don't mean a woman. Was there an activity or an interest that, for some reason, was jeopardised.'

'Politics for a politician might be, I would say, such a passion.' Harry suggested.

Donald Leyland nodded his agreement.

'Yes, if the man's a politician, a political disaster could be the trigger. However that opinion, although quite possibly accurate, is not very scientific.'

'So another political catastrophe might cause him to kill again.'

'It's quite possible. He may feel no emotion about the deaths but the effect of the killing may rid him of a mental turbulence caused by his political failure.'

Leyland stopped for a moment and then added.

'Of course, the catalyst could be something very simple and insignificant like Rosebud.'

Harry smiled. He understood the reference and in his mind the image of a child's sleigh burning in the furnace in Xanadu came rolling back.

And that was it for the moment. The Superintendent was pleased with the meeting. He had liked Donald Leyland and their discussion was, he felt, worthwhile. The interview had given the detective somewhere to go.

From Billy's profile of Hogan, Harry could extract the dismal points of the man's political life.

When he returned to the station Harry carefully read Lynch's potted biography of Hogan again. There were certainly some very black spots. The question now was whether some of these occasions occurred simultaneously, with the wanton killing of the young victims.

The body of Sarah Malone had been discovered in the bus shelter on the promenade in Salthill, in Galway on April 21st 1999 and Dan and Emer scoured The Connaught Tribune and The Galway Advertiser for anything to link Dennis Hogan to the city on that day.

It didn't take long to make a connection. It was an advertisement in The Advertiser announcing the opening of the new Ardnamara Fitness Centre on April 20th. The advertisement stated that the former minister, Dennis Hogan would do the honours and cut the tape.

Of course, this could be a coincidence but that was unlikely. It proved nothing. The ceremony had been scheduled for noon. This was more than half a day before the girl had died. Hogan could have been well gone from the city by midnight, but it was a first brick.

There were no further references in the Galway papers and the Limerick back issues had not yet arrived, so for a while there was nowhere to proceed to on that front.

Billy's project would require a great deal of routine effort. From the St. Dominick's College Annual he had discovered that there were ninety five boys in the class of '74. Don Kinsella had estimated that the Union would have contact numbers or addresses or both for about seventy per cent but he could not vouch for their accuracy. Informing the Union of a change of address would not have been seen as a priority by the old boys.

It hadn't taken Kinsella more than a few minutes to get a printout and it produced seventy three names. That meant they were roughly twenty short.

Billy needed to work out how exactly to approach the chore. He knew that telephone research frequently produced poor results and that face to face interviews were far more productive. He had three questions that needed to be asked. Who were your close friends in your final year in St. Dominick's College? Did you keep in touch with them after you left school? Did you associate with them in university?

With a bit of luck, this might produce a useful short list.

Harry liked Billy's initiative and he decided that the team would concentrate on Lynch's plan of campaign in the morning. He would give each of the team a quarter of the names and they could spend the day finding answers. Harry knew it would take more than one day to track down and question seventeen or eighteen people but it was certainly worth a lot of effort to get a list of Hogan's school and college chums.

Later, Harry and Emer shared a few drinks after work. They were in Bakers pub and were intending to go to a film in Dún Laoghaire afterwards. They had both found the day intense. It was frequently like that in the early stages of an investigation.

Emer had decided the time had come to give Harry a push in terms of their relationship.

'I think we'll go to Galway for the weekend,' she invited.

Harry Tinto didn't say no.

Angela Forde had died on April 21st 1982. Her body had been found on waste ground on the banks of the Lee. Like the others, it appeared she had been chosen at random.

Hogan was a political nobody at the time. It would be most unlikely that his presence in the southern capital would merit a mention in the publications of the city, but you never knew and you never dismissed any possibility on a hunch alone. Dan was instructed to acquire the back issues of those papers.

The next day was Thursday and everything was concentrated on Billy's project. Harry had allocated himself just one visit. He wanted to see Hogan. He wanted to talk to him to get the feel of what he was dealing with.

There was no difficulty with an appointment. Harry had indicated that he only needed a couple of minutes of the minister's time. He was fitted in to the great man's schedule at ten o'clock.

As he entered the minister's office, Dennis Hogan stood up and walked to the door to greet him.

'Good morning Superintendent, I believe I may be of some assistance,' he said pointing to the seat for Harry to take.

'I only need a minute of your time, Minister. A criminal matter we are investigating relates to the class of '74 in St. Dominick's

College. We are interviewing as many old boys as are available and asking two questions.'

'Then ask me.' Hogan invited.

'Who were your closest friends in your final year in school?'

'I had plenty of good friends. John Doyle, Mark Dowd, Martin Devereaux, Michael Hutton and Peter Francis were my closest. I'm still close to Peter, Martin died recently and I've lost touch with Michael and Mark.'

Harry took a note of what Hogan had said and then put his paper away.

'Did any of them go to university while you were there?'

'They all did except for John. He went to the states, he died, I believe, a few years back.'

'That's all Minister, thank you for your time,' The detective said.

Harry stood up to take his leave.

'Can I ask what the investigation is about?' the minister asked.

'I'm afraid I'm not a liberty to give you any details but we have an issue with one individual from your year and we need to discover who his friends were at the time. However, I can tell you his name is not on your list.' Harry said truthfully.

At the day's end progress had been slow. There had been wild goose chases to homes from where St. Dominick's old boys had moved on. The total number of interviews carried out had been eleven. Billy and Pete had done three apiece, while Emer and Dan had grabbed two each and Harry's one.

Of the ten, only one had included Dennis Hogan on his list. That individual was Mark Dowd. It was interesting to note that Dowd had also included Doyle, Devereaux, Hutton and Francis.

Hutton had also been interviewed and his selection seized everyone's attention. He had listed five close friends and again these included Doyle, Dowd, Devereaux and Francis. Hogan was not included. The fifth name was a Conor Canavan.

Harry's plan for the next day was for more of the same. Dan, Billy and Pete would continue with the list, making a special effort to see Francis and Canavan. Emer would try for a few old boys in the morning but she was taking the afternoon off. She was going to Galway with her gentleman friend for the weekend.

The Friday morning was bright and the forecast for the weekend was excellent. Emer was on the road early. She had packed her bag and was ready for work and the weekend. She had made some appointments the previous day. The first was arranged for nine o'clock.

Frank Dwyer was a medical man and was waiting for her when she arrived. He was a little anxious at the request for information about his boyhood friends and was keen to know the reasons for the inquiry. Emer gave the standard reply about not being able to divulge details of a case.

The man had clearly something to hide but no hint of what was concealed was given. He co-operated as much as he could and the names of the close friends she was given, were new to her.

Then she took a chance.

'Do you remember a boy called Martin Devereaux?' she asked.

'Certainly I do,' Dwyer replied, 'he died recently. We were in the same class together but I didn't know him well. I suppose we were acquaintances, I only met him a couple of times over the years at St. Dominick's functions, anyway we associated with different groups.'

'Who might he have had an association with?' Emer pressed.

'There were three or four of them in the clique, Hutton, yes Michael Hutton, Dennis Hogan the politician, a lad called Dowd and another called Francis. If I remember correctly, they were a very close knit bunch.'

'Have you met any of them over the years?' she asked.

'I see Hutton from time to time, socially. We both live in Foxrock and we have a drink together occasionally. He's a teacher in St. Dominick's.'

Frank Dwyer had become more talkative. Once attention was focused on others, he had relaxed significantly. Emer wondered what the man had to hide.

Emer thanked him for his time and asked him not to relate the details of the meeting to others. She was satisfied that he would remain silent. He would not wish the focus of police attention to be trained on him again.

Billy met Peter Francis early as well. Francis was the chief executive of Francis Media Services and the policeman's first impression of the man was not favourable. Billy's impression was that Francis was intoxicated with his own importance and was irritated that his valuable time was being taken up and wasted with

50

silly queries about his days in St. Dominick's College and the friends he had there.

That attitude was a mistake. Billy Lynch did not take kindly to people making his job more difficult. More than that, he interpreted the poor attitude as a lack of respect for the force of men and women who daily jousted with the forces of darkness to protect society. In a word, Billy got thick and took on the role of the dumb flat footed copper. He slowed everything down, his questions, his note taking, even his speech.

Francis was feeling a rising frustration. He knew he had been stupid and he knew what the policeman was doing. He decided to make amends.

'Officer,' he began, 'I owe you an apology. I was rude and arrogant when you came in. Can we start again?'

Billy, pleased with the man's change of attitude, tidied up the business in a matter of minutes. Billy knew that the businessman had learned a lesson and would not try to belittle a garda again.

The meeting had produced nothing new but it did confirm what they had already been told by others, that the group consisted of Devereaux, Hogan, Francis, Hutton and Dowd.

It was Monday morning and as she watched Dublin bay from the DART on her way to work, Emer thoughts were not on the day ahead but on the days gone by. It had been a wonderful weekend for both of them. They had made that ultimate leap in their relationship and had landed safely. The Ross Lake House Hotel had been exceptional, perfect for them. It was nestled in woodlands at the foothills of Connemara. It was small and exclusive, welcoming and personal.

On the door step was Oughterard, the gateway to God's country where the panoramic vistas gave a sense of freedom which enriched the soul. The discovery of places full of beauty and wonder such as the road from Louisburg to Leenane and the sudden reminder, to both of them, of an elderly cleric who, just months before, had, in this wonderland, been dispatched to his Master by a still unidentified hand.

As the DART pulled into Connolly station Emer's thoughts jumped back to the present. There was a killer to be caught and it was her business to help get him.

The papers had arrived from Cork and by noon, Dan had read through most of them. He had concluded that there was nothing of value in them. However he knew that Harry would not be happy with one reading of them and someone else, probably Pete, would also get the job. Dan knew that Tinto would read everything himself as well.

Harry sat over a coffee in the lounge of the North Star. He needed time for his daily think tank. He liked lists and this was what he was doing. Tabulating everything they had.

There was a tenuous link with Hogan in that the suspect had been in Galway on the day that Sarah Malone had died. That was all they had. They were investigating many strands of inquiries but that was where they were at this point.

They really had very little. Even the Devereaux letter had been written on a word processor so there was no absolute certainty that the academic was the informant. They were, Harry knew, a very long way from making a charge and much further from the securing of a conviction.

Harry's thoughts then turned to his conversation with Donald Leyland. His suggestion was that a great passion jeopardised could have been the catalyst that triggered the killings. Clearly politics was what consumed Hogan and there were significant disappointments in his career. These failures, judging from Billy's research, seemed to coincide with the killings. The death of Angela Forde in Cork in eighty two had occurred within a few weeks of Hogan's failure to win a seat in a general election. Ninety-nine saw Hogan sacked from the cabinet. Shortly afterwards Sarah Malone died in the shelter on the promenade in Salthill. Then five years later Miriam Nolan's killing in Limerick occurred just a week after Hogan failed in his attempt to win the leadership contest with Matt Dolan to become Taoiseach.

Joanne Boylan's case was different in that Hogan's political career had not yet begun but his failure to secure a university degree a few weeks earlier could have been responsible for setting in motion a train of events that led to the young woman's death.

It was all speculation and maybe coincidence but Harry felt it was fact. However there was nothing in it that the Director of Public Prosecutions would listen to.

There was, at the back of Harry's mind, the fear that the killer might strike again. It looked unlikely. Hogan's career was flourishing and there were no signs of any political turbulence on the horizon but one never knew. A day can be a long time in politics. So Harry would watch out.

Devereaux's confession had said that there was a group of friends drinking in the International Hotel on the night of the murder, but only some of them had participated in the disposal of the body. This made them accessories to the girl's murder and liable for prosecution and a lengthy jail sentence. If the members of this group could be identified, either conscience or self preservation might motivate them to give the necessary evidence to send Hogan to jail for the rest of his life.

Harry had spent the best part of an hour with his coffee, his lists and his thoughts. He was pleased with his endeavours. The priorities would be to continue tracking down the drinkers in the International Hotel and to have a closer examination of the original investigations into the deaths of the other three victims.

The Limerick papers were examined by both Dan and Emer. These consisted of an evening paper and two weeklies. Almost immediately they hit the jackpot. Dennis Hogan had attended a symposium on 'Economic Development' in the University on the night that Miriam Nolan had died. He was photographed at the function along with the student organisers and other guests. It was progress and it suggested, even more, that they were on the right track. However it proved nothing.

Harry was pleased. The investigation had moved forward a small step. It was not at all surprising that there was nothing from Cork. It was just too long ago. But they had a link with both Galway and Limerick, maybe they could copperfasten that connection. He decided that this was a job for Pete.

If Hogan had been in the cities overnight, he would have stayed in a hotel. Hotels keep records. There was a good chance that the Limerick hotel would still have their reservations database. After eleven years, the hotel in Galway where Hogan had stayed was unlikely to have a record. But it was worth a try. Cork would be out of the question.

The investigation had gone as far as was needed with the lists from St. Dominick's College's Past Pupil's Union. The squad was convinced that the people they were interested in were Dowd, Devereaux, Francis and Hutton. Canavan had been disregarded as he appeared only on Michael Hutton's list.

There were four new players in the game and all Harry knew about them was that they were friends of Dennis Hogan during his college days. He knew that the chances were high that one or more of them had been drinking with the minister on the night that Joanna Boylan was killed. Maybe one of them helped with the disposal of the body. Maybe it was one of them who drove the stolen vehicle to Wexford.

Who knows?

He needed more. He needed to know about these men and their history. The more information that was available when a witness was being interviewed, the easier it was to press the right buttons. Harry feared that these men might never face prosecution for being an accessory. It all happened too long ago.

It wouldn't take long to assemble biographies on the four. Harry had a gut feeling about Hutton. It was clear that Hutton was part of the crowd that Hogan had hung round with. They had all mentioned Hogan, they had all mentioned Hutton. Why hadn't Hutton mentioned Hogan. There must have been a reason.

It was coming close to nine o'clock when Harry finally got home. He was at ease with the world. Emer and himself had a meal and a drink together after work and that was for him a perfect codicil to a busy day.

There was nobody at home. Rita could be anywhere, Fiona, he knew, was spending the night with Sinead. Fiona's baby was not due for another month yet, but her health was good. There had been no complications apart from the blood issue. She was continuing to work and had made no decision about what she was going to do once the baby arrived.

Harry had made it clear to her that she and his grandchild were welcome to live with him for as long as she wished but he was putting no pressure on the girl. What he wanted was what she wanted. It was that simple.

His plan for the remainder of the evening was uncomplicated. He would watch the news, enjoy a glass of wine and look at an old John Wayne movie. However the second item on the news at nine o'clock put a spanner in the works.

Taoiseach Matt Dolan was being interviewed and he appeared to be suggesting that there might be a cabinet reshuffle in the not too distant future. The station's political correspondent, in his evaluation of the interview, was saying that this was a bolt out of the blue. He said that the development had not been expected. He went on to speculate about possible demotions and which newcomers might be expected to be in the frame, with a chance to sit at the captain's table.

Dennis Hogan's name was not mentioned.

Of course, Harry knew what it was all about. Dolan's motivation was to get Hogan off his front bench. He would be distancing himself from any political fallout that there might be, when and if his minister was arrested and charged with murder.

Harry would have to stop the reshuffle. The Taoiseach had absolute authority in deciding who would or would not serve as a minister in his Government. Harry would have to tell Matt Dolan that there were worse things for the country's leader than having one of his ministers charged with murder.

Emer had heard the news as well and had called Harry.

'Did you see the news Harry?' she asked.

'Yes, a reshuffle could put the cat among the pigeons as well as putting some young girl in harm's way. But not to worry, I know the man and he is a decent individual. He won't put his political wellbeing before someone else's life.'

Rita had turned up, and seeing her father on the phone, crept into their lounge and turned on the television.

When Harry returned to his armchair Rita remarked, 'No marks for guessing who was on the phone, Dad. You know, the two of you are behaving just like teenagers instead of a couple of broken down geriatrics.'

Harry laughed.

'She might be right about that,' he thought.

Hogan's old school friends had savoured success in their professional lives. There was a solicitor, an executive, a professor and a teacher. The teacher was the odd man out. He was easily at the very bottom of the ladder when it came to the accumulation of wealth. Interestingly, the teacher was Michael Hutton and he worked in St Dominick's College, his own alma mater.

It wasn't that he was impoverished, it was just that relative to his friends, he wasn't at the financial races. It appeared that he maintained little contact with most of his former friends and was not part of their social circle. It wasn't that he avoided them. He couldn't. They had sent their sons to St. Dominick's and over the years, he had taught some of them.

Harry had little difficulty in deciding that Hutton would be the first he would talk to. He would not wait any longer, he would interview him the next day if possible.

Nothing had been found in any of the newspapers that had come from Cork relating to Dennis Hogan. Dan had gone through the papers first. Then Emer had repeated the exercise and the result of her efforts was the same as Dan McCarthy's. Nobody had expected anything to be found.

Harry saw the southern papers stacked neatly on Emer's desk and started browsing through them. He was sure it would be a waste of time and effort but he liked to check things out for himself. It wasn't that he distrusted the work of others, he just liked to see for himself whenever that was possible. Harry found nothing.

Then something struck him and he started back at the papers with a vengeance. Paper by paper, page by page until he found what he was searching for. It was in the morning paper published on the day of Angela Forde's death. It was a local news item and it referred to a convention of auctioneers being held in Cork that week. There wasn't much in the piece except to report that the event was taking place and that the convention was located in the Monument Hotel and that the Minister for the Environment would be addressing the delegates that day.

Dennis Hogan had been an auctioneer with Murphy, Kelly and Murphy before he had won a seat in the Dail. It was possible that Hogan had been a delegate at the event. If so, Harry wondered whether it would be possible to show that twenty eight years ago the suspect had the opportunity to kill Angela Forde in the southern capital?

Halpin was assigned to find out about the auctioneering firm.

'Pete, I want you to be careful when checking this out. Give them no information and get the answer effectively to two questions. Was the firm represented at the convention and, if so, who were its delegates? I think you should stress the importance of not talking about the inquiry to others.'

Harry was confident that Pete would abide by his instructions but thought it necessary to give him a gentle reminder on the observation of some of the basics of police work. When a garda reached Pete's age, the routine of all the years could lead to a sense of déjà vu which often resulted in carelessness. The same, he knew, applied equally to himself.

Emer had arranged for Harry to meet with Michael Hutton at Hutton's Dean's Grange home at five o'clock. She didn't know who he was taking with him but expected it to be someone other than herself. It was an important interview and she felt that it would require somebody with more experience than her.

Harry didn't see it that way at all. He was taking Emer because he wanted to convey to Hutton a softer and less threatening persona. But Harry had a problem. There was a possibility that Hutton was party to the crime and therefore liable to prosecution. It was his duty to caution Hutton at the commencement of the interview and if Harry did so, it was practically certain that the teacher would insist on his rights and request to consult his legal representation. Then Harry would get nothing.

As Emer and Harry were driven to Dean's Grange, the detective had not yet made up his mind about how he would approach the interview.

When the car turned into the Kill Abbey estate Harry knew it was 'make his mind up time' and he asked his driver to pull in. Emer wasn't coming and the squad car was not going to pull up in front of the Hutton's home. No wagging tongues in the neighbourhood, would probably be appreciated by Hutton and his family.

It took Harry almost ten minutes to find Hutton's house as the estate, although pleasant and well maintained, was a warren of small cul de sacs and the numbering of the houses had not been entrusted to one who liked matters simple and uncomplicated.

Michael Hutton answered the door and invited Harry in. Harry was surprised with Hutton's appearance. He looked significantly older than his years. Harry got the sense that he was not in good health. He had a gaunt jaundiced look and yet he was, Harry knew, younger than himself.

'Mr. Hutton,' Harry began, 'there are a number of things I need to discuss with you before I ask you any questions. I think, in your own interest, you would be well advised to say nothing until I have finished.'

Michael Hutton nodded both his understanding and his agreement.

'The reason for the cloak and dagger approach is fairness for you and an attempt to catch a killer for me.'

Hutton nodded and Harry continued.

'Over thirty years ago a young girl was murdered in Bray and her body dumped in a ditch on a country road. The girl's name was...'

'Joanne Boylan,' Hutton interrupted.

'I have some reason to suspect that you may have been involved after the incident. I believe that this involvement related to the disposal of the girl's body, the tampering with evidence and the shielding of the perpetrator from justice.'

Harry paused for a moment then continued.

'What I want is for you to tell me what happened that night. You will note that I have come here alone so there will be no one to corroborate what is said. I will take no notes and there are no recording devices. I bring to your attention the fact that, so far, I have not cautioned you. The bottom line is that I have no interest in bringing a prosecution against you or the others that participated in the concealment. Simply, I want the killer. Now, I don't have any authority to say that there will be no prosecution but I think it is reasonable to say that if you talk to me, that anything you say is not admissible in court as the circumstances surrounding this conversation are highly questionable.'

Harry was finished. It was now up to Hutton. Harry could sense that the teacher was in two minds.

'By the way Mr. Hutton, you won't know this but Joanna Boylan was not the only one.' Harry added.

That disclosure seemed to seal the issue. Clearly, Hutton had never considered that there might have been other killings and it struck him to the core of his being.

'How many altogether?' he asked weakly.

'Four that we know of, all girls of Joanne's age and spread over thirty years.'

'If we had spoken up then...' Hutton didn't finish the sentence but Harry knew what occupied his mind.

'Yes, it would have made a difference but now I want to stop it and to do that I need your help.'

Michael Hutton began to relate his version of the fateful Saturday night.

'I think, I remember every moment of that evening, still to this day. It haunts me always and it's true to say that the memory of it has never been far from my conscious mind all through the years. There were eight of us in the International Hotel that evening. We were drinking and the plan was to go to a disco later on. We were all students and all male. There was myself, Hogan, Devereaux and Dowd. There was Doyle, Peter Francis, a chap called Canavan and an English fellow called Stephen Jones. It was a good night and the conversation eventually became quite philosophical, in an immature kind of way. One of the topics was the perfect crime. We didn't take any of it seriously. At least seven of us didn't. Dennis Hogan wasn't winning his argument and he got a bit agitated about it. The discussion petered out and we went to the disco. Four of us left the club together at about two o'clock. Dennis Hogan was waiting for us outside.'

Hutton stopped.

'I need a coffee, before continuing,' he told the detective, 'will you join me?'

Harry nodded his agreement. He didn't want to say anything that might break Hutton's train of thought. The teacher was back within a minute after putting on the kettle and he continued.

'The other three were Francis, Dowd and Devereaux. Hogan wanted to show us something. He led us back down towards the seafront and up into a cul de sac. We walked up the lane towards a parked car. When we got to it, a Ford Cortina, Hogan announced with a flourish that he had committed the perfect crime. He told us that he had killed the pretty barmaid who had served us that evening in the hotel. None of us believed him and this angered him. Then, with the gesture of a circus ringmaster, he opened the boot of the Cortina and we all saw Joanne Boylan.'

The kettle was boiled and the story was interrupted again and for a second time Harry Tinto said nothing.

Five minutes passed before Michael Hutton continued.

'We were all stunned, shocked and lost. Somehow Dennis convinced us to assist him. I don't know now why I helped, just as I didn't know then. I don't know where Hogan found the car or who owned it. It certainly wasn't his. Anyway he decided to dump her body away from the alleyway. I think it was one of the others who suggested the road to Roundwood. It was probably Francis.'

Hutton paused to sip his coffee and then continued.

'Devereaux had his mother's car and we decided that Dowd and I would go with him. Francis went with Hogan in the Cortina. We met no traffic on the road, not a single car from Kilmacanogue to the spot where we left her. By this time the enormity of what I had got involved in was to the forefront of my mind but I didn't say anything or do anything. The five of us lifted the body from the boot of the car and laid her on the roadside. Someone, again I think it might have been Francis, suggested that we should put her behind a hedge. We all lifted her over the hedge into the field. There was a ditch and we laid her there. Hogan threw his jacket over her face.'

Hutton was quiet. Harry felt that he no longer cared about his own situation. He was just relieved to have told his secret to someone.

'Afterwards Francis and Hogan drove off together. They said later that they torched the car down in Wexford but I don't know whether that was true or not. Nothing was ever the same again for a gang of boys who had grown up together. Over the following months I drifted away from Hogan and Francis.'

Michael Hutton was silent for a moment.

'Outside of St. Dominick's I don't think I've had any real contact with either of them. I was friends with Martin Devereaux up to his death. I meet Mark Dowd from time to time, we're not close but, I think, we're still friends.'

And that was it.

Harry hadn't learned a great deal more but Hutton had put flesh on the bones of Martin Devereaux's written confession. Michael Hutton was alive and Harry wondered if the teacher would put what he said into a statement.

As he broached the subject, Harry felt as if he were walking on eggs, a slip and the spell would be broken.

'What do you think that you'll want to do next?' Harry asked.

60

'There is only one thing to do. You said yourself that there were other deaths, not unlike Joanne's, and you wouldn't have mentioned it unless you thought that there was a connection. And who knows what could still happen.'

'Personally, I'm convinced that all four deaths were perpetrated by the same killer,' Harry said.

'Yes, I think it's time to finish this off.'

Hutton stopped for a few seconds.

'Was it Martin's death that stirred up interest in the case again?' he asked.

'There was an unsigned confession, but we feel certain it was him.'

'Good old Dev.'

And Hutton left it at that.

Harry had a hundred questions that he wanted to ask, but for that he needed official surroundings, so he limited his curiosity to one further question.

'How did the others react to the situation after the initial shock of seeing the body?' Tinto asked.

Hutton thought for a few moments before replying.

'Martin's and Dowd's reaction was, I would say, the same as my own. Francis on the other hand seemed to revel in the adventure of it all. I don't think that he fully comprehended that a life had been snuffed out and that he was part of an attempt to protect a killer. He went in the car with Hogan and afterwards they left together. But really that's just speculation, I just don't know.'

Before Harry left, he made an arrangement for Hutton to make statement in Store Street the next day. They set the time for midday to allow Hutton to arrange to have some legal representation available. He assured Harry that he would not have second thoughts, no matter what his solicitor advised him.

As Harry walked back to where Emer and the squad car waited he realised that he had been with Hutton for more than an hour and a half but it had been time well spent. All being well he had a witness who would testify that Dennis Hogan, politician and minister of government, had admitted to killing a twenty old girl three decades before.

61

The case for him could be closed within a few weeks and the thoughts and plans for a holiday away with Emer re-emerged as he walked up the shallow incline towards the car.

Dan McCarthy was having a hard time getting adjusted to the routine of the daily grind. The summer had been a rollercoaster of a ride until the third Sunday in September when the hopes and dreams, the effort and training had culminated in a focal point of just seventy minutes.

The All Ireland football final was and is the most important sporting event for Irish sports fans and there are always winners and losers. Dan was a winner but not just an ordinary victor. He was the conqueror, the hero, who from far outfield in the dying seconds of an extraordinary contest grabbed victory with an unbelievable point.

Dan didn't know it then but he would carry that point into every room he entered for the rest of his life. A moment of genius, perpetrated when it mattered most, had made him a legend and no matter what heroics he performed on the field of play in the future, it would not matter. That point scored at four fifty nine on that Sunday in September was all that would ever be remembered.

In the past weeks the celebrations had been continuous but now he knew that he needed to get his mind back on his work. His trip to Galway and the few quiet drinks with local colleagues had started to get him thinking. He was a garda. He had chosen to be one and it was still how he wanted to earn his living. He had a job that he liked and there was a game that he loved. He didn't need the constant back slapping, the free drinks and the even freer women. The content and the quality of his professional life were not going to be determined by one magical moment of time.

Dan had noticed that Harry Tinto had given him nothing significant to do in the current case. He had been given no responsibility. He had been allowed to clock in and do it by the numbers.

Harry was a wise old copper and knew the effect that the victory would have had on him but Dan knew as well that, in time, the Superintendent would expect him to get back on his professional feet and make this return known.

Dan knew that he could not turn his back on all the activities that eminated from winning the All Ireland but he would limit his participation to weekends. There was little point he reckoned in

62

winning a medal and losing his career if he could keep and treasure both. He would have a private word with Harry in the morning.

The squad car dropped Emer and Harry off at her Glenageary home. She would make something for them to eat.

'Emer, a thought just struck me. I don't know whether you can cook or not. I want you to note that I have a sensitive stomach,' he joked.

'Don't worry, Dún Laoghaire hospital is just down the road, I think I might be able to get you there in time to save you. Now make yourself useful and do something constructive. You can take this bottle of wine and open it. The glasses are in the top press on your right and then disappear into the garden and read the paper. I'll get on with it here.'

Harry poured a glass of wine for each of them and leaving her with her wine and a kiss, he did as he was told.

The next morning was alive with the scent of the kill. Harry outlined to the team his interview with Michael Hutton. He repeated the details of Hutton's version of the killing. He figured that he hadn't forgotten much. He told his crew that Hutton had agreed to make a statement. The teacher was also prepared to testify.

They all knew they had little else that would be admissible in court and as a bonus, Hutton's evidence would implicate Dowd and Francis.

Harry would take Pete with him to the interview. It would, he had decided, be low key. There was no need for any high powered techniques, Hutton was not hostile. His contribution was voluntary.

By twelve fifteen Michael Hutton had not arrived or phoned but Harry was not unduly worried. Hutton had been solid about his intentions the previous evening and he doubted that Hutton's solicitor would be able to dent that resolve. Hutton had made up his mind on the issue and the detective figured that he was the kind of person who stuck with his decisions.

By one o'clock there was still no show. Harry asked Emer to make a phone call to Hutton's home. She was back inside two minutes.

'There's bad news, Harry.' She said.

'Has he had a change of mind?'

'No, it was a neighbour who answered. Hutton has been taken to hospital. He is alive but she doesn't know what's wrong yet.'

Harry rested his head back against the wall.

'Did she say where he was taken?' he asked.

'St. Vincent's,' she replied.

'Ok, lets go and see,' he said to Emer. 'As for the rest of you, I'll see everybody here about three.'

It took a couple of minutes to organise the transport but they were on their way within ten. It was about one thirty when they got to the hospital, to be told that Hutton was no longer in casualty but had been admitted to a ward.

A medical team were still working on Hutton when Tinto and Emer arrived and were not available. Harry then saw a small group of people standing silently at the end of the corridor. Harry reckoned that they were Hutton's family and went over and introduced himself. They told him that their father had had a stroke but the doctors didn't yet know the extent of the damage. They had been told that he was not in any immediate danger but if there was another stroke that could change everything. Harry thanked them and returned to Emer.

'It doesn't look good, but it's too early for the doctors to say. Let's go and get a sandwich, I'm starving.'

Then a voice from behind announced.

'Good afternoon, Mrs. Ryan.'

Emer and Harry turned to see a tall young man in a white coat.

'Well hello Adrian, how are you?'

Emer introduced Harry to Adrian Maguire. He had been at school with Emer's son Brian and had, in his school days, been a regular resident in her front room.

They chatted easily about the past and the present for a few minutes.

'By the way Adrian, you wouldn't know anything about the patient behind the screens. His name is Michael Hutton.' Emer asked.

'Yes, we're waiting for the consultant. The guy is in bad shape but it's too early to make any prognosis yet.'

They chatted on a little longer.

'He seems a nice young man.' Harry remarked.

'Always was.' Emer said when the doctor had gone.

'Yes, just what I need for Fiona,' Harry joked.

'Have you heard anything more about her blood problem?'

'They tell me all is under control, that there is no risk as long as it is being treated,' he replied.

And Emer left it at that.

A sense of disappointment permeated through the incident room with the news from St. Vincent's. They were back to the beginning. There was little chance that an approach to Dowd, similar to what Harry had made to Hutton, would succeed. Dowd was a solicitor and his legal training and experience would tell him not to admit to anything. He would feel safe. Who would give evidence against him? Certainly not Hogan or Francis.

Billy Lynch figured that Peter Francis was certainly not going to testify against the politician. Francis ran a public relations company and Hogan's department was its principal client. This had always been the case. When Hogan was in government Francis always worked for his department. They were close, not only did they work together but they socialised together as well. Where Hogan went, so too did Peter Francis.

Harry decided that they would go back to the beginning and start all over again. Very little effort had been put into re-examining the three later cases. Most of the time and energy had gone into Joanne Boylan. Now the unit needed to spread its wings.

However there were only five of them and that was not enough. They needed another body now. Harry knew the time had come to talk to Donal Joyce again.

Billy was having the time of his professional life. There had been no incidents with colleagues and senior officers. He knew his work was good and that it was being appreciated. He knew too, that this would last only as long as he was working for Harry Tinto. Retirement, at the end of the year, loomed closer.

These thoughts had been resurrected a few days earlier with the circulation of plans for a retirement party for Jack Doyle. Doyle had joined the force at the same time as Billy and Tinto and they had been friends ever since. Doyle had cancer and, although not life threatening, it was sufficiently debilitating for him to have to call it a day. Billy thought that maybe if things remained the same he could stay on.

He had not kept these thoughts to himself but had shared them with his wife, Lily. Her support carried just one caveat.

Only with Tinto.

Nearer the time Billy would have a word with Harry.

For the moment Harry decided not to spread their resources across all four cases. They would concentrate their efforts on Galway and Limerick. Billy and himself would look after Limerick, the other three would concentrate on Galway.

What had been done to date in relation to Sarah Malone's death was very little. The files, with all the statements, had come from Galway but, other than the pathologist's report, nothing had been checked.

Dan seemed to take charge and this caused nobody a problem. Pete was a plodder and a good one but he and responsibility had never been close, so he was happy that Dan took the wheel. Emer, with her very limited experience was not, she knew, in the race.

Harry had noticed the change in Dan. He was up and running and Harry likened it to Dan's attitude to his football. A new season had opened. There was a championship to be won but this would only be achieved by being focused, driven and a great deal of hard work.

Dan was back.

Harry decided that he would send Billy to Limerick to sift through what had been accumulated in the five or so years since the girl had died. There was, he noted, a significant difference between this and the three other cases. Many of the gardaí who had worked on the original investigation were still active and still stationed in Limerick.

As these thoughts passed through his mind, he thought that Emer's ex-husband might have been involved in the case.

Harry knew Limerick quite well and was familiar with the location where the girl had been found. She had been discovered in a car park behind the Swan Centre, which was only a stone's throw from O'Connell St. This surprised him a little because, in the other cases, all the bodies had been found away from the town's centre. Harry needed more. Hogan may have been in Limerick for the event at the university but had he stayed the night and if so where? There were several fine hotels in the city, sufficiently worthy to host a prominent government minister like Dennis Hogan.

The Castletroy Hotel might be the most prestigious. It was very close to the university campus and convenient for the return journey to Dublin. However there was a 'but'. The hotel was some distance from where Miriam Nolan's body was found and the minister would not have had his own personal transport. He would be using his ministerial Mercedes with a garda driver. He could not utilize this if his agenda included murder. Neither could he have used a taxi or borrowed a car. That could have prompted questions.

The Century Hotel was, on the other hand, just an easy stroll from the Swan Centre and another of the city's premier establishments. Harry would get an occupancy list for the night of the killing.

The Superintendent was put through to the hotel's manager without delay. There would be no problem with his request. The computer would still have that information stored. He would e-mail the list within an hour. And he was true to his word.

The list contained forty three names. None of them was that of Dennis Hogan.

Billy was still with him.

'No luck with the Century, Billy,' Harry said passing him the e-mail.

'I'll try the Castletroy.'

Harry received an equally co-operative response from the Castletroy. Their list of ninety guests did include Dennis Hogan.

Tinto turned to Lynch.

'Billy, Hogan stayed the night. The Castletroy must be two or three miles from the Swan Centre. I want you to check the distance when you get there tomorrow. If Hogan is the 'perp', there are some questions that need answering. How did he get to and from the centre of town? How would he have known where to look for a solitary young girl? A deserted city centre car park is not where you would expect to run across someone in the dead of night.'

There was nowhere further to go for the present. He would join Billy in Limerick later in the week but they would talk again the next day.

Dan decided to drive to Galway that evening. There was nothing to keep him in the capital until the morning. His renewed enthusiasm had given him a buzz which he was enjoying. Pete would follow him by train in the morning.

Dan had already been in touch with the Chief Superintendent in Galway who had arranged office accommodation for Pete and himself for the few days. They had been assigned an officer to assist them for the duration of their stay.

It was six o'clock when Harry got to see Donal Joyce. A lot had happened since they had last met. Joyce was concerned when Harry explained to him that the killing may not be over and that it looked very likely that Dennis Hogan was the perpetrator. They had a witness who had indicated his preparedness to testify. However, the witness had been felled by a stroke and his medical prognosis did not look encouraging at the moment.

'Donal, I need some additional manpower.' Harry asked.

Joyce knew that if Harry Tinto needed something then he needed it.

'What do you need?'

'One body.'

'I'll assign someone to you in the morning. You know it is a bit ironic, here you are investigating the deaths of four young girls with only five gardaí working on it and if a thug is murdered by an associate tomorrow there would be more than thirty officers involved.'

'I suppose that what is immediate seems to matter more,' Harry replied.

'Yes, for some.'

'But not Donal, for you or I.'

Billy was on the road by five o'clock the following morning and was walking into the Henry St. station in Limerick just before eight. At the same time Harry was walking from the DART to the incident room. Emer was already there.

So too, was Ellie Kennedy.

Ellie Kennedy was waiting for Superintendent Tinto. Last night she had been assigned to him by Donal Joyce.

Harry was not surprised when he saw her. Joyce never wasted any time. When he said he would do something he would do it there and then. Harry introduced himself and told Ellie to get a coffee for herself and write a resume of her career in the force to date. He would be ready to talk to her in half an hour.

With the others away there was only Harry and Emer. They had spoken the previous evening and he had told her that he had asked Joyce for some help.

'Now that we have the extra manpower, I'm going to pull you back from the Galway case and get you and Garda Kennedy to work on the Cork killing. That will mean all four cases are active.'

Emer knew they were operating with severely limited resources which made progress slow and success questionable, but that's the way it was. However there was a silver lining to such a dark cloud. It gave someone like herself, with practically no operational experience, the opportunity to manage and be responsible for strands of an investigation that otherwise would never have come her way.

Angela Forde had been murdered in Cork in February 1982. And that was all they knew about the case at this point. Harry had established that there had been a convention of estate agents in the city at the time of the killing and it was possible that Hogan had been a delegate. Pete had been assigned to find this out but Emer didn't know how far he had got with the inquiry. She would check with him later. Emer would go to Cork, probably the next day, and she would take her new associate with her. There, they would trawl through the aged paperwork and see if any of it would be useful.

Harry read through Ellie Kennedy's career summary carefully. He was pleased. In addition to the usual routine assignments, she had been attached to a specialised task force digging into a white collar fraud for some time. And while it wasn't murder, it was, in Harry's opinion, significant experience.

Billy took to his task like a duck takes to water. He waded through the statements and other data with a vengeance. Within three hours, he was ready with his first report to Harry.

He had been allocated a room to work in and local members of the force were keen to be of assistance. There was, of course, a curiosity about his presence. An old case, dormant for years, was being re-opened by a Dublin unit, which was being led by the legendary Harry Tinto. Billy was quizzed by the locals about what new information had come to light but Billy was not talking.

He just passed the buck.

'Look, I can't say,' he said, 'but Tinto will be here either tomorrow or the next day, you can ask him then.'

However, the put off did not dampen their interest or curb their helpfulness. A young girl had been killed on their patch and no one had answered for the crime. Now someone else was looking at the case and this was good. The fact that a killer was walking free among the community stuck in their craw, so any assistance that was sought would be forthcoming with alacrity.

Superintendent Tim Ryan was particularly pleased with the participation of the Dublin unit. The original investigation had been his and he viewed the failure to bring Miriam Nolan's killer to justice as his. He knew that everything had been done correctly. It was just that the killer left no traces. The thought of a perfect murder on his watch upset him.

Ryan had never met Harry Tinto but he had heard of him almost all his working life. He was the kind of policeman that recruits hoped they might become and wished they had been when they were old men. Ryan would be pleased to assist him.

Of course, Tim Ryan had heard of Harry in a different context recently. His daughter Nuala had been the informant. She had told him that Emer and Tinto were close friends. Ryan was happy for Emer. He was pleased that she had found someone new and pleased that it was someone of substance.

The phone rang. It was Billy.

'Harry, I'm just reporting in. Henry Street is being very helpful, everything I need, I get. I have started with the statements made at the time. We knew that Miriam was a student at the university but what we didn't know was that on the night of her death she had attended the function that was attended by our friend. There is no doubt about this. She was in the company of some friends. Afterwards, she appears to have gone to a drinks reception for the speakers and the committee. The event had been arranged by the Economics Society. Miriam was one of its members.'

Harry listened without interruption.

'Billy, I'm coming down to Limerick tomorrow. I'll take the early train. Can you arrange for someone to collect me at the station?'

Harry was pleased with what Billy had told him. It had placed Hogan in the same room with the victim on the night of her death. This, of course, didn't prove a thing. He called Billy back and asked him to check, if it was known, how many guests and committee members might have attended the reception.

7

Emer liked Ellie Kennedy. She was enthusiastic and cheerful, motivated and bright. She was also tall, blonde and very pretty. They would get on well together.

Emer knew that the first thing Ellie needed was to be inducted into the case. The two women slipped away to the bar of the North Star Hotel for a coffee and a briefing.

It was clear to Emer very quickly that her new colleague was well and truly up to speed. She grasped things quickly and had the gift of insight.

It is about a mile from the Galway railway station to Garda headquarters and Pete was with Dan shortly after eleven. All the data that was available on the case had been collected together. Dan had spent the morning sorting through the accumulated material.

Sarah Malone had died twelve years before but there was nobody in the station who had been stationed in the city at the time. Therefore there was no emotional connection with the unsolved killing as there was in Limerick. Of course, there were retired policemen, like Michael Baker, still living in the city.

But Dan was news. Newly raised to the status of legend, a hero in blue jeans, he was welcomed. The younger officers saw him as one of their own. Their superiors saw him as the perfect role model for the troops.

There was nothing instantly revealing in the statements that Pete and Dan read through. Sarah Malone was a student. She was in the second year of an Arts degree and lived, at home, with her parents. Her home, on Threadneedle Road, was just yards from where her body had been discovered. Sarah had been to a pub with friends and got the late bus home afterwards. She had been alone. The bus driver had distinctly remembered her. Sarah had definitely got off the bus at the end of the promenade. She had been the only person to do so at that stop. The time, the busman reckoned, was probably about 11.45.

It had been early the next morning when her body had been discovered and the pathologist put the time of death as almost certainly before midnight. When Sarah Malone alighted from that bus her young life was over.

There was no obvious motive for the killing. She had not, as Michael Baker had said, been sexually assaulted. The forensic evidence did not help much. Any material found in the shelter could have been left by any occupant and there were no traces of anything useful found on the girl's clothing. The knife had been found. It had been dumped, in some shrubbery, not far from the scene. The killer must have been very confident that it wouldn't incriminate him or lead anyone in his direction.

There were traces of blood on the knife and analysis showed that it belonged to the girl. There were no prints on the handle or the blade. As for the murder weapon itself, it was just an ordinary kitchen implement which could have been found in most households and available in any hardware shop in the country.

It was only speculation but the original investigators figured that the girl could have been alone at the bus stop in town and had been seen by her killer. He could have followed the bus out to Salthill. He might have observed her getting off the bus and seized his opportunity.

Harry had one issue he needed to deal with. He needed to talk to Matt Dolan. One phone call and one hour later, Harry Tinto was ushered into the Taoiseach's private office.

'Do we need to be alone, Harry?' he asked

'Yes, Taoiseach,' the Superintendent replied.

Without being asked the two men who had been with Dolan left the room.

'Take a chair Harry,' Dolan said pointing to one in particular, 'what can I do for you?'

Harry told him of the events that had taken place since they had last met. He briefed Dolan about Hutton and his story that Hogan was a killer. He repeated the psychiatrist's opinion of what might have triggered the murders. He told the Taoiseach about the deaths in Cork, Limerick and Galway which coincided with Hogan's political troubles.

'And that brings you to my proposed reshuffle. You want me to cancel it because you think it might be the catalyst for another killing?' the Taoiseach asked.

'No, I'm not requesting that you cancel it, just that you don't touch Hogan.' Harry replied.

'It's really the same thing, isn't it?' Matt Dolan said

'I suppose it is.'

Later Harry phoned St. Vincent's Hospital and was told that there was no change in Hutton's condition and that the prognosis was still not encouraging. Any downward spiral in the teacher's health would lessen any hope for justice and retribution for Joanne Boylan.

The Cork investigation was going nowhere at present but that might change with Emer and Ellie's trip down south. Limerick was showing some promise. Billy had been able to put Dennis Hogan and Miriam Nolan in the same room on the night of the killing. However there was, so far, nothing to suggest that they had even spoken. There had been no contact with Dan in Galway but Harry knew it was full speed ahead in the city of the tribes. Dan would be in touch when he had something to report.

Pete had been on the train to Galway when Emer phoned him. He told her that he had attempted to check whether delegates from Murphy, Kelly and Murphy had attended the convention in Cork in eighty-two but there was no one there who could help him. He had been told to try a Matt Keane who was now retired. Keane had been with the firm for years. It was suggested that he might be of help. Pete had an address and a phone number for Keane and passed it on to her. Emer phoned Matt Keane and an appointment was made for Ellie and herself to visit him in the afternoon.

The phone rang, it was Dan.

'An idea struck me, Harry.'

'Go ahead tell me.'

'The post-mortem report stated that there were no injuries to Sarah Malone's body other than the knife wounds. Now if the girl was accosted at the bus stop, she would not have gone willingly with a stranger to the shelter. She would have struggled. She would have fought back and would have needed to be restrained. This would have left tell tale signs, either cuts or bruises, certainly something. Harry, this suggests to me that she walked willingly to the shelter and logic would indicate that she was acquainted with her killer.'

'Not just that, but she knew him well enough to trust.' Harry added.

'I have been going through the statements and reports but so far there is nothing to suggest that the issue was raised in the original investigation.'

'Is there much information about the girl's family?' Harry asked.

'There was nothing special about them. Well educated, and reasonably well off. There was another girl and a boy in the family and both were younger than Sarah. They were fourteen and twelve at the time. The father was an accountant. He's dead now. Her mother was a housewife. There isn't anything unusual about the family.'

'Right Dan, I think we need to know more about the family, the father in particular. What was his background in both his business life and his private life? Was he political and if so what was his party affiliation? Were there any links to a particular senior politician? You know yourself what we are looking for.'

They were finished.

'Get back to me later, Dan.'

Matt Keane was almost seventy five years old but had the appearance of a much younger man. He had worked for Murphy, Kelly and Murphy for more than thirty five years and fifteen years ago he had taken early retirement. He hadn't severed his links with the old firm and filled gaps for them periodically, which was frequent enough.

Matt Keane led his callers into his sitting room and offered them coffee which they accepted. Emer viewed the acceptance of the coffee as a token of respect towards the old man. He would accept them more easily and it would encourage him to provide them with all the assistance he could.

'We're carrying out an investigation into a crime that took place in Cork in nineteen eighty-two. A young woman was brutally killed. The annual auctioneer's convention took place in the city during the same week. It was, I understand, held in the Monument Hotel.

What we're looking for are the names of the delegates your firm might have sent to the event.'

Keane was silent for a moment.

'It's a long time ago,' he started, 'I was there myself, I went every year then, but anything I told you would only be guess work. The various conventions are now merged together in my mind and what I might attribute to one year might in fact relate to another. Sorry.'

He had no more to add.

Emer was disappointed but she knew she could not expect Keane to remember details of something that had taken place twenty nine years before. They talked on for a few minutes, finished their coffees and then took their leave.

Matt Keane stood at his open door as Ellie closed the gate behind them.

'Wait,' he called to the gardaí.'

A minute later the three were back in the old man's sitting room.

'All my life, I have kept things. What I mean is that I keep documents. I have probably every payslip, every bank statement that I have ever received. I probably have a copy of any business letter that I have written. I don't think I have thrown out a single instruction manual. What I'm getting to is this. At these conventions there was always a gala dinner on the final night. There was a tradition that everyone at a table would sign the menus as keepsakes. All the delegates from a particular firm would be at the same table. I almost certainly have the eighty-two menu somewhere.'

Keane promised to search for the card. He would phone Emer when he had located it.

Emer smiled when she remembered the coffee. It was important when dealing with older people to remember that they operated at a slower pace than her generation. She wasn't quite sure whether it was a feature of old age or simply that they had lived and worked in an age when speed was not as important and life was significantly more leisurely.

The women were hardly back in Store Street when the call came. Keane had found the menu 'card' as he had called it. Ellie would collect it within the hour.

Billy was puzzled. His thoughts had turned to how Hogan might have travelled from the Castletroy Hotel to the quays and back again on the night of the killing. The only safe way, to avoid recognition, was to walk. As physical activity and Billy were not constant companions he arranged to have a young garda assigned to take a leisurely stroll from the quays to the hotel. The garda completed the outward journey in forty five minutes. To Billy a ninety minute walk late at night by a government minister on the off chance that he might encounter a young woman alone did not fit. There must have been some other explanation. There must have been some form of transport used.

Questions came to mind quickly. Did Hogan link up with Miriam at the university? Did she have car? If that were the case then surely someone would have seen them together. The best bet remained that Hogan had chosen the girl purely at random and that it was entirely co-incidental that they had both attended the same drinks reception.

Dan had been with Harry at the previous meeting with Michael Baker and the retired sergeant was delighted to meet again the young policeman who had scored that glorious winning point in Croke Park a few weeks before. However there was business to be discussed. Dan asked if any attempt had been made to establish whether Sarah had known her assailant. Baker shook his head.

'I was only on the periphery of the investigation. I was the sergeant in the Salthill station and was not privy to the details of the investigation. However, I never heard anyone refer to the murder as anything other than a random killing.'

Dan accepted what the older man said and asked.

'What do you know about the girl's family?'

'I knew Mark Malone well. He died a few years ago. I don't think the man ever recovered from Sarah's death. He was an accountant and a prosperous one. He was well liked and very interested in football, golf and politics. He ran for Galway Corporation and won a seat about twenty five years ago. Mark was not interested in expanding his political career but he was involved locally up to his death.'

There was nothing else that Michael Baker could help him with.

Dan knew it wasn't a lot.

Could Mark Malone have known Dennis Hogan? Dan didn't know. There were thousands of party supporters all over the country and few were ever likely to get close to a minister or a former minister. It might be worth inquiring if there had been some form of political relationship between Sarah Malone's father and Denis Hogan

The day had opened several new avenues to be explored. This required Harry to re-assess the assumptions that they were operating under. They had presumed that the victims had been chosen at random but both Billy's discovery and Dan's speculation put that assumption seriously in doubt. It could still have been the case that the killings were random and that Sarah Malone and Miriam Nolan were just in the wrong place at the wrong time. Maybe the killer didn't even recognize his victims and the links were just coincidence. There were an awful lot of maybes.

Then there was the menu with all the signatures. There were fourteen in all. Among them was a name that was familiar to Harry, that of Dennis Hogan.

Before going home Harry again checked with St. Vincent's Hospital. There was still no change in Michael Hutton's condition.

The Superintendent was not one for anxiety and worry. He had been a fatalist all his life and lived by the maxim that what will be, will be. There were things, in most of our lives, which were unalterable, so one got on with life as best one could.

The west pier in Dún Laoghaire played host to only a few walkers on this bright and optimistic late autumn evening and nobody took any notice of a lone man submerged in his thoughts.

The grapevine was efficient in its delivery of gossip and the St. Dominick's College branch had been working overtime. It was known that the police were investigating something relating to the class of '74. They had interviewed some forty old boys and then had discontinued the exercise. It would be reasonable to assume that they had found what they had sought.

Although the investigators had indicated nothing relating to the purpose of their questions, it was obvious, that whatever it was, related to a time gone by. Why else would they want to know about particular friendships that blossomed and perhaps faded thirty years ago.

Dennis Hogan thought it was very possible that he, a Government Minister, was the subject of the inquiry. He had killed a girl in cold blood. But why should it crop up now? It didn't make any sense. Sure, there were four others involved at the time. There would be no reason for them to make waves now and besides Devereaux was dead. Hutton, he had heard, was hospitalised with a stroke and largely incapacitated. They would have been the only possible informants.

The other two had too much to lose by opening their mouths. After all this time, he could only vaguely recall the details of the night but he could still feel the powerful pleasure of his first kill. To have within his power the life of another and the ability to snuff it out at will was, for him, the ultimate satisfaction. He could no longer remember the girl's face but he could recall clearly the sensation he felt as the long blade pierced the flesh of her young body. He had committed the perfect murder. There had been nothing to connect him to the girl. That had been the beauty of it. No link, no suspicion, no charge and no conviction.

Now, as he walked, he knew there had been an error. In the intervening years, scientific progress had produced DNA testing and that was where his mistake lay. He shuddered when he remembered throwing his jacket over the dead girl's face. Today, DNA analysis could establish beyond doubt that he had worn that coat.

Then there had been the other killings. They had all been an attempt, on his part, to recapture the pleasure of the first kill and although he found them enormously satisfying, they lacked the perfection of the original. But they had all served their purpose.

The minister had reached the end of the pier and had made the turn. He had come to the conclusion that there was nothing to worry about. Sure his DNA was on the jacket, he would have a simple explanation for that. No problem. He would make a call and see how Michael Hutton was responding to treatment.

Harry needed a sounding board, somebody to listen to him as he spoke his thoughts. Ellie Kennedy was the only one around so she got the job.

'Ellie, I'll be doing some talking, it's my way of thinking a problem through so if you notice something wrong you tell me. If something isn't clear, ask.' Harry said before starting.

'Ok. Four killings all told. All were girls either late teens or early twenties, anyway all young. The four were killed with a long bladed knife. The pathologist Davitt says that it is probable that they were all killed by the same man. This individual was tall, probably over six foot in height and strong. We know that Dennis Hogan is tall and strong. He had opportunity. Devereaux's note, which is confirmed by Hutton's conversation with me, says that the politician killed the Boylan girl. The menu signature confirms that he was in Cork on the night of Angela Forde's death. On the day Sarah Malone died, Hogan opened a fitness club in Galway. The opening ceremony was around midday, we don't know whether he stayed the night or not. Finally, on the evening that Miriam Nolan died he was in Limerick at a function in the university. Afterwards, he attended a drinks reception at which the victim was also in attendance. The suspect stayed the night at the Castletroy Hotel which is about three miles from the crime scene.'

Harry stopped.

'Anything so far, Ellie?'

The young garda shook her head.

'Right, what I've said are facts. Now let's see what we've been speculating about. I think there are two issues here. We speculated earlier that the victims were chosen at random, but now we're not so sure. It seems probable that Miriam would have been introduced to the guest of honour at the reception. In Galway, it is possible that the girl's father could have met Hogan on the day Sarah died. If so, could Hogan have met the daughter as well?

'The killings could be random in the sense that the killer took advantage of an opportunity when it presented itself. He didn't go and seek out his victims.' Ellie injected.

'Yes, that seems to be an option. Hogan certainly didn't seek out Joanne Boylan. She was just working in the bar where he was drinking. Miriam Nolan was attending a lecture that the minister was attending. And we don't know about Sarah or Angela.'

Harry paused for a while and turning to Ellie he said.

'There are questions arising from what I've been talking about that need to be examined, so take a note of them. If I speak too quickly, slow me down.'

Harry waited for the young garda to get a pad.

'First, had Angela Forde any connection with the auctioneers' dinner or the hotel in which the function was held? Did Sarah Malone meet Hogan on the day she died? Did Hogan stay on in Galway after performing the opening ceremony? If he did, where did he stay? How did the politician spend the afternoon and the evening? Where, relative to the university, did Miriam live? Was her home near the scene of her killing? Was there any suggestions, at the time, that might account for her being in the city centre at that hour?' Harry was finished.

'Anything you'd like to add, Ellie?'

'Yes, just one question,' she replied, 'why would a government minister carry a kitchen knife with him?'

'A very good question, Ellie. Why indeed? It wouldn't be easy for him to acquire one. He couldn't go into a shop and just buy one like an ordinary citizen. Yes, where did the knife come from?'

'Another thing, that struck me earlier. We know that Joanne Boylan was not killed where she was found and that Sarah Malone died in the shelter but I've seen nothing relating to where the other girls died.'

'Another good question, Ellie. Take a note of it.'

Emer and Ellie were collected from the train and were in Cork's Anglesea Street station by eleven o'clock. Thirty minutes later they were ensconced in their work. The folders of statements and reports had not been seen for more than twenty nine years and the eyes, that once scrutinised them, were now all dimmed.

As both women browsed the mountain of paper, looking for a place to start, Ellie spied a folder marked 'Angela Forde'. She passed it unopened to her colleague and Emer started with the victim.

Angela Forde had been born in Cork and had lived all her nineteen years there. Her parents were professional people and financially very comfortable, enabling them to provide well for their children and have high aspirations for all of them.

Angela was their youngest and was in her second year at University College Cork, as it was then called. She was an Arts student and was studying French and Spanish. Her hope, to the dismay of her parents, was to become a teacher. However, there was an independent streak in her. Angela had wanted to contribute to her own maintenance and had taken a job at the Monument Hotel. Her work there was on a casual basis. She served in the bar, the dining room and at functions, a few evenings a week.

On the night of her death Angela had been working in the hotel. She had been part of the crew that had serviced a function. This had been the gala dinner at the conclusion of the auctioneers' conference. She had not worked late. As far as it could be determined, she had left the hotel a little after eleven thirty. Nobody had left with her and no one had seen her leave.

Her parents knew she was working but had no idea what time she would be finished at. This was not unusual, as it can be difficult sometimes to gauge when a function will disperse. Her standard practice was always to take a taxi home. This was not difficult as the Monument was a large hotel and taxis were constantly dropping off guests right into the shank of the night. The investigation had shown that she was familiar to many of the drivers but nobody had seen her the night she died.

Angela Forde's body had been found on a rough patch of ground about two miles from the hotel by a group of girls on their way to school.

The original investigators believed that if they had found the means, that took her to that lonely place, then they would find the killer. However their inquiries proved fruitless. Hours, days, weeks were spent in an attempt to find some lead that might open up an avenue of investigation but there was nothing.

The forensic evidence had shown that the girl had died elsewhere and had been dumped. Nothing had been discovered that would assist the police in their inquiries.

The police had developed a number of theories about the case but after analysis most of them were eliminated. However the detectives remained certain that the hotel was a key element in the case. They had been convinced by everyone, that Angela would not have left the building to go hunting for a taxi. It was simply not her way.

They reckoned that she must have met her destiny in the hotel. Was it someone she knew? Was it a stranger? There was no way of telling. She had not been seen leaving so it was possible that she might have been driven out by car. The hotel car park was underground. It was large, with a capacity to house a hundred cars and there was access to it from inside the hotel. Unfortunately there were no CCTV cameras at the time. It would have been a simple matter to come or go without being seen. So too, it would have been easy to leave and return unobserved.

There was little further in the report. It was clear to Emer that it was really a summary of everything that was known. It was an act of the closing of the book, the washing of hands and moving on.

Ellie had spent her time reading through the scores of statements that had been taken. This included the people who worked in the hotel on the night, hotel guests, friends, relatives. The police had been thorough, they had contacted all the guests who had checked out the morning after, but had come up with nothing. Ellie saw the name of Dennis Hogan on the list of those, from whom the police had taken statements.

It was concentrated work reading those old documents. Emer and Ellie were both conscious of the necessity to be fully focused on the reading. Browsing was dangerous. It implied reduced concentration and this increased the possibility of missing something.

There was little reason to stay in the southern capital. There was no one there who was involved in the original investigation. The documentation could be shipped to Dublin.

Neither woman could see any light at the end of the tunnel for Angela Forde. All they had got for their efforts was a confirmation of what was already known. There was nothing new, nothing at all. They would get the late train back to Dublin.

Dan had noted Harry's questions. Did Hogan remain in Galway for long, after opening the fitness centre and if so where did he stay? If he didn't remain in Galway where did he go from there? It would be difficult finding answers without showing his hand, but that was what he was expected to do.

He decided to go directly to the top and in Galway party circles that would be their sitting T.D., Seamus Druhan. Dan was in luck. Druhan was in town and would see him.

'Mr. Druhan, the background is this. You might remember about twelve years ago a young girl was murdered in Salthill.'

'Yes, I remember it well,' the politician interrupted, 'Sarah Malone, I knew the girl well. Her father and I were very good friends. How can I help?'

'New information has come to light and the case has been re-opened. As you would expect, after so long, there is a new team at the helm and we have gone back to basics. Sarah's father was involved in local politics. Was there anything of any consequence happening in Galway on the day she died? Could you tell me anything you can recall about the day?' Dan asked.

'It was a big day for us here. I was just a councillor in those days. Dennis Hogan was in town to open a fitness centre. He had just recently been relegated to the back benches. He had taken his demotion badly. The real purpose of his visit was to gauge what kind of support he had in the west. Maybe, it was with a view to a heave against the then Taoiseach. I don't know.'

'Was Sarah's father involved in any of this?'

'Mark was a strong supporter of Hogan, so was I for that matter. There were meetings all over the place after the opening. They went on until it was quite late, maybe ten or ten thirty.'

'And Mark Malone was at some of them?' McCarthy asked.

'He was at them all. We both were.'

'Who else would have been involved, apart from the two of you?'

'Well Hogan had a bit of an entourage from Dublin with him. There was always a few of them around. I can't remember who they were. Of course, there were many of our local cumann members there, probably most of them at some point or another.'

Dan was slowly edging his way towards the two questions he needed answers to.

'As far as you can recall did Malone meet his daughter at any stage during the day?'

'Hogan was staying in the Ardilaun Hotel and the cumann had organised an early dinner there. Sarah and her mother attended, I remember talking to both of them. How could I forget? It was the last time I saw the girl. I had known Sarah all her life. They would have left early, probably when the meal was over. Certainly before nine.'

Dan had what he needed but continued with questions deflecting attention away from Hogan. Ten minutes later, he thanked Druhan for his time and his assistance.

Harry was pleased with what Dan had discovered. In a sense it was all sown up. They had Dennis Hogan tagged to the extent that he had the opportunity to kill all four young women but knowing it and proving it were two entirely different things. They had no evidence, other than Hutton's testimony, to link the minister to any of the deaths. It was still a long way to the halls of justice.

Mark Dowd sat at his desk. There was nothing very pressing to be dealt with that morning. This was just as well, as the solicitor's mind was far away. He had met some friends from his school days and the conversation was dominated by the Garda interest in the class of '74. When he had been asked by the detective about his school friends he thought nothing of it, but now there was a haunting sense about the inquiries. The lads had been full of it and they had placed much importance on the fact that only about half the class had been questioned, before the process had been aborted. It was either that the police had decided that the investigation was futile or that they had found what they had been looking for.

A few discreet calls told him that all those who had left the deceased Joanne Boylan in the ditch on the lonely road to Roundwood had been questioned. It didn't look good.

Dowd could sit no longer. He felt the need to move so he left his office. He had no idea where he was going. He just felt the need for solitude and the opportunity that it gave him to think.

Logic told him that there was little need for the anxiety that he felt. It was not possible to bring such a case to court after thirty years. There were no witnesses. There was no evidence and besides he had not killed the girl. All he had done was to help lift the girl's body from a car and transfer it into a ditch. But Dowd knew that this was all rubbish. He had been aware of a killing and had not reported it. He had been part of a conspiracy to protect a killer and that was the plain truth of the matter.

Another call was the real source of the anxiety that he was feeling. It had been confirmed to him that Joanne Boylan's case was being investigated again and the officer in charge of the new investigation was Harry Tinto.

Dowd and Tinto's paths had crossed a few times over the years and although they could not be described as acquaintances the knowledge that Tinto was on the case was not a good omen.

Mark Dowd had driven north out of the city and found himself in the car park of Newbridge House near Donabate. As he wandered the grounds of that old stately home he pondered his options.

Self preservation is in the nature of animals and the human being is no exception. Exposure would signal the end of his legal career. He would certainly be disbarred and his lucrative practice would evaporate if its principal was shown to be a criminal. It was not the financial aspect that worried him. He had accumulated sufficient wealth for a lifetime. It was the shame of it all. He could see no way of avoiding the disgrace that a Tinto success would bring down upon his head. It was an ignominy that would tarnish those he valued most. A wife, for whom he cared dearly, a son and daughter at university and another son still in St. Dominick's College, would all be tainted by his fall from grace. He would play a waiting game. He would do nothing for the present, other than to distance himself from Hogan.

Harry's train was approaching Limerick where, for the next few hours, he would be concentrating his attention on Miriam Nolan.

As he stepped onto the platform a tall man in his late forties stepped forward with an outstretched hand.

'Harry Tinto, I presume, I'm Tim Ryan.'

'Glad to meet you, Tim. Emer has spoken of you.'

Billy had done a lot in the twenty four hours he had been in Limerick. Much of it had been relayed to Harry over the phone but that did not prevent Lynch repeating it. And Harry listened.

It had been the opinion of the investigating team that Miriam had not died in the car park where her body had been discovered. Their reasoning was simple. The kind of wound that had been inflicted would have produced a great deal of blood and very little had been found at the scene. It was clear that death had occurred elsewhere and she had been dumped where she was found.

Why had she been moved? There was only one answer. If the girl was found where she had died, her killer might have been compromised. Her removal was an act of self preservation.

The original team had never discovered where the girl had died. They had presumed it had been somewhere between the university campus and the car park. The distance was about three miles and there were not many places, in the area, with sufficient privacy for a killing. Extensive searches drew a blank.

Interviews, taken at the time, failed to locate anyone who had seen the girl leaving the drinks reception. The function had lasted about an hour and five witnesses had spoken to Miriam. They had all known her well and there was nothing different about her manner or humour that evening. She was enjoying the event, just like they themselves were.

There was plenty of other information collected but it was more background material than anything else. It simply didn't move the case forward.

Harry hadn't needed to travel to Limerick for this information. Billy would have reported it to him perfectly. The purpose of Tinto's visit to Limerick, was to talk to and consult with some of the men and women who had been involved in the original investigation.

Tim Ryan had headed that inquiry and he had gathered the ten remaining officers together for Harry to meet. Harry had found his girlfriend's ex-husband a decent and likeable sort.

Ryan still felt the frustration of not being able to do anything with the case. The killer had left behind no evidence to mark his passing. Ryan had felt that Miriam Nolan had been picked out of the blue to satisfy some pervert's thirst for blood. Ryan could not see any other reason. Miriam had not been sexually molested. It had to have been random selection.

Harry was not surprised that Tim Ryan did not question him about the renewed interest in the case. If their roles had been reversed he would have been the same. If he was not being told, there must have been a reason and no senior policeman wants to be refused an answer.

Ryan was open and realistic and did not fudge the issue. The facts were the facts and in this case the investigators were never at the races. A month after the girl's death they were no closer to their quarry than they were on the day the body had been discovered.

The meeting with the ten detectives provided no insights into the case and as with Tim Ryan, Harry could sense a feeling of unfinished business.

Afterwards Harry, accompanied by Billy, was shown where the girl's body was found. Then they were driven to the Castletroy Hotel and the university campus. Harry wanted to be familiar with the geography of the case.

For most of the return journey to Dublin, Harry was lost in his thoughts while Billy snoozed the hours away. There was something wrong with their thesis. Billy's research had thrown a spanner in the works. Up to this, they had wondered how Hogan might have got from his hotel to the city centre and then back. How did the minister get the body from a place unknown to a car park in the middle of the city?

And why? Yes, there was something seriously flawed in their assumptions. Hogan could not have left his hotel, acquired some transport, made contact in some way with the deceased, killed her, dumped her body, disposed of the vehicle and made his way back to his hotel. It was possible but not without leaving some trace behind.

So where did that leave them? The Superintendent would think about it later because, like Scarlett O'Hara, for Harry Tinto tomorrow was another day.

8

Harry had a late lie in the following morning. He was tired after his long day in Limerick. It was important that he remembered that he was no longer a young buck with the energy levels that were appropriate to men of Dan's fitness and age. It was a matter of not being careless and foolish.

Besides, there were family matters that needed a little attention. He was thinking of Fiona in particular. It had been sometime since they had had a serious chat about plans and hopes, dreams and wishes after the arrival of his grandchild. It wasn't that he was curious, it was just concern for a daughter, who was about to become a mother and who had nobody else to turn to. But the best laid plans can go awry and by the time he got up Fiona had gone to work and no conversation had taken place.

On his way into Store St., Harry stopped off at St. Vincent's Hospital. He wanted to check on Hutton's condition. He needed to assess whether there was a possibility that the teacher was ever going to be in a position to give evidence. If that was out of the question, then it was better to know the worst now rather than relying on his recovery.

Harry had little difficulty in getting an interview with the doctor in charge, an English consultant, a Doctor Kirby York.

The detective found it refreshing dealing with this man. When asked a direct question the physician gave a straight answer. In Hutton's case he didn't pretend to know. Anything could happen. Over a period of many months he could recover sufficiently or he could be struck down with another stroke in the morning. The message was clear without being certain. There was nothing to rely on. Harry would have to forget about Michael Hutton. He would need to find another way to slay his dragon.

Everyone was back from their travels and, apart from Billy, all were in the incident room when Harry arrived. They were waiting for their leader. Without him, they were akin to a rudderless boat and they needed to be directed about what to do next.

Harry sensed their emptiness when he entered. He knew what it was. It was a lack of experience and only time would teach them that valley periods, when everything appears to be a dead end, were all part of the routine of an investigation.

For an hour, he listened to each member of his team report on their activities. He had heard most of it already but he wanted everyone to have the full picture. When everybody was finished Harry gave them his analysis of the situation.

'From our efforts yesterday and the day before, I have come to the conclusion that we are going to get nowhere in Cork. The examination of the files by Emer and Ellie has shown that the original team had nothing. We're going to let Cork go. I don't like doing this but with our limited resources, I feel that our efforts might be more productive with the Limerick and Galway deaths. It's not that we have much but there are connections that we can examine and they might, with a bit of luck, lead to something.'

Harry stopped for a pause as Billy joined them.

'The same goes for Bray. Without Hutton there is no case and it seems unlikely that he will ever be sufficiently fit to give credible evidence.'

It was Billy who interrupted.

'Harry, is there something about the Miriam Nolan case that you've got some misgivings about?'

Although it could not be discerned, Harry smiled to himself. Billy was a cute old fox. Tinto had not shared his insights and doubts with him. It was just experience and observation, astuteness and cunning that allowed Billy access to his boss's thoughts.

'Yes, Billy you're right. If Hogan is the Limerick killer I cannot see how he could have done all that was required without transport. We know that he was using his state car for the visit and he wouldn't have access to it without his driver.'

'So where does that leave us, Harry?'

'Two possibilities spring to mind and neither fits our interpretation. One, Hogan is not the killer and two, he had help.'

'The second option could indeed fit in with the Bray death,' Emer interjected, 'Hogan presented his achievement to his friends in that instance.'

'Maybe, he liked an audience.' Ellie added.

'Yes and if that is the case,' Dan added, 'there is a likelihood that his collaborator is one of the old friends. This is, of course, all speculation based on our ignorance of how Hogan might have carried out the deed in Limerick without transport.'

'Dan, it is only speculation at this time,' Harry said 'but it may be a scenario that we might need to look at later. However, for now, we won't change direction.'

It was Ellie Kennedy who made the next contribution. Harry had developed a sneaking regard for the young garda and encouraged her to give her view.

'There is one possibility that I think we have overlooked in relation to Dennis Hogan in Limerick. He could have committed the crime, our problem is the transport. There is the possibility that he stole a car. If he had the knowhow, he would have little difficulty finding a vehicle in the hotel car park or nearby. Remember a car was stolen in Bray.'

Harry was pleased. Ellie had spent time in the traffic corps and would have been involved with that kind of crime daily. It just went to show that the man on the beat or in the squad car was often more in tune with the basics than the high flyer. It was a forgotten unimportant little thing but it could be the straw, that finally broke the killer's back.

Within seconds, Billy had disappeared and everyone knew, without being told, what he was up to. A phone call direct to Tim Ryan and the wheels were set in motion. An hour would tell them whether a vehicle had been stolen from the hotel or its vicinity on the night that Miriam Nolan had died.

Harry had a feeling that the chances were high.

It had taken the Limerick station less than the hour to come back with the information Billy had requested. There had been three car thefts in the city on the night in question. One of which had been from the car park at the Castletroy Hotel. It was a Toyota Corolla and it had belonged to a staff member. The vehicle had been found the following morning less than a mile from the hotel. It had been burnt out. Nobody had seen it being taken. Nobody had witnessed the fire.

This new information seemed to put them back on track. It would support their original contention that their suspect was the killer. But they were no closer to making a charge. Everything they had was highly circumstantial and would not carry any weight in a court of law. There weren't any witnesses to the killing. There was no physical evidence. There was no DNA that could connect any of the victims to the killer. They really had nothing.

They could continue indefinitely making very little progress. The investigations needed a catalyst and Harry knew what it could be. There was Mark Dowd, Peter Francis and Dennis Hogan. He would interview all three in connection with the killing of Joanne Boylan.

Mark Dowd practiced his law from an office in Ballsbridge. It was a prosperous practice in an affluent part of town. He did not expect to see the police knocking on his door. Dowd had anticipated that contact could be made at some point. He felt it would be made discreetly and in keeping with his position in both the legal world and social circles.

Harry Tinto was not easily impressed. A crime was a crime and Harry made little distinction between criminals. To him, Dowd, for all his status, was just another person who had broken the law.

Harry and Billy were kept waiting, five, ten then fifteen minutes. If the solicitor was with a client then there was no complaint but if Dowd had some other agenda, it was a different matter.

Harry was getting impatient.

'Is Mr. Dowd with a client?' Harry asked the receptionist.

'No, but he is just finishing something.' She replied

'Then you just tell him if he is not out here in sixty seconds I will arrest him and take him to Store Street for questioning.'

The woman was taken aback and Mark Dowd appeared within thirty seconds of the woman entering his office and quickly ushered the gardaí into his private domain.

Harry was having no time for the pleasantries and niceties. He got to business straight away.

'Mr Dowd, we are, at present, investigating the death of Joanne Boylan who was murdered in Bray more that thirty years ago. We have reason to believe that you were involved in an aspect of the crime and we want to interview you in relation to that. We need to caution you that what you say may be taken down and later used in evidence against you.'

Dowd was stunned. He was being treated like a common criminal. He was a suspect in an investigation into a serious crime. This policeman was allowing nothing for his status or standing. He was playing this according to the rules and making absolutely no concessions. Mark Dowd was thinking fast. He was thinking like a lawyer.

'Mr Tinto, I would like to invoke my right to a legal consultation.' He said.

'Clearly I have no difficulty with that. I want you to be at Store Street station tomorrow morning at eleven o'clock.'

As the two detectives left the shaking solicitor, Harry turned to Dowd and said, 'Think long and hard. Reduced professional and social standing is one thing but a long custodial sentence is another matter altogether.'

Harry didn't want to interview him yet. There was nothing that Dowd could tell him that was not already known to the policeman. He wanted him to stew, to worry, to think and to walk his floor late at night. He wanted Dowd to replace Hutton as his witness. He wanted the solicitor to send the politician to jail for the remainder of his life. In the morning, he would postpone the interview. It would help soften Dowd, whose current bewilderment would soon turn to anger and then arrogance until finally he would realise that his best interests lay working in tandem with the angels.

Apart from the emotional reaction of his visit, Harry wondered if Dowd would contact either Francis or Hogan. He thought not. Dowd knew the law and they could not help him. In fact, consulting with the others could be construed as conspiring to interfere with the justice system. It was one thing for him to conspire to hide a crime when little more than a boy, to do so now would be a different matter altogether. No, Dowd would not contact the others.

Harry had not quite decided who he would interview next. The situation was different as Francis and Hogan had remained not just friends over the years but also close colleagues. When one was contacted the other would know and nothing would be a surprise. It would be better to put Hogan on the back foot. The best that could be gained from Francis was what Hutton had already told him and what he expected Dowd eventually to confirm, when the solicitor had thought matters through.

When would he make contact with the minister? Harry figured the sooner the better. Emer had checked it out and Hogan was in town and would be for rest of the week.

Ellie liked Dan and when she had been assigned to assist him, she felt her heart beat a little faster. Dan, she knew, was a catch. He had become a legend on the field of play but it was not just that that had attracted her to him. It had, of course, helped when they first met those few days ago but she had quickly found that he was more than that. He was serious and hard working, good humoured and courteous. These qualities emerged within hours of their meeting and now they were working together. She wondered what place she occupied in his thoughts. It wasn't that she was blind to her own striking attributes. She had always known that she was a good looking woman. She couldn't see it in herself but was aware that others viewed her in that way.

She knew little of Dan's personal life but felt it safe to presume that he didn't suffer the lack of female company. She wondered, what if?

Emer had had little time with Harry since his return from Limerick twenty four hours previously. She wondered what his impressions were of Tim, her ex husband. She expected they had got on well. Tim Ryan would have been helpful to both Billy and Harry. She would have expected nothing less. Their marital difficulties were personal. Tim had always been a good policeman.

She hoped that Harry liked her former husband but she didn't know why it was important to her that he did. Maybe it was because there had been a time when she had loved him and had seen in him many fine qualities. Perhaps it was that when she had chosen to marry Tim Ryan she had chosen a good man, and just because their marriage faltered didn't mean that her judgement of people had been flawed. Anyway she would find out soon enough.

Billy was still annoyed with himself that he hadn't thought of the possibility that a vehicle might have been stolen. It was an obvious consideration. It's not a difficult thing to hot wire a car but, of course, a person needs to know what they are about with alarms and immobilisers now standard on most models. So it makes life easier if an older vehicle is taken, such as the one stolen from the hotel grounds on the night of the killing.

The burnt out wreck was now long gone to the Valhalla where all cars eventually make their way. At the time it would have been a simple case of car theft and no association would have been made with the death of Miriam Nolan. There would have been no forensic examination carried out. There would have been little point as the fire would have destroyed everything.

Billy ran the sequence of events through his head. If Hogan had taken the car then everything fitted. The probability was that the minister was the killer.

The murder weapon had never been found but it was known to have been a knife. Earlier in the inquiry, it had been suggested that a person as identifiable as Hogan would not risk recognition by buying a knife in a hardware store. Someone was certain to remember. But acquiring a sharp knife would not have been a difficult task.

Billy considered the possibilities, as any blade was not sufficient. It required something pointed and sharp. Hogan could have taken something like it from his home but that was unlikely. These killings did not seem to have been premeditated to that extent. Sure, murder was in mind when the act was perpetrated but not twelve or more hours before.

It seemed that the crime stemmed from a sudden passion to kill. The weapon could easily have been acquired during a meal in the hotel. A steak knife would fit the bill admirably. It would be pointed and sharp. Had Hogan availed of room service on the evening of the killing? Had he eaten a steak? There was no way of knowing or was there?

There were other ideas that Billy Lynch considered but he kept coming back to the sharp steak knife. It had everything going for it. It was easy to acquire and it was an effective tool. If Hogan had availed of room service, it was simplicity itself to return the knife from whence it had come. He could have left his tray, with the murder weapon, outside his door, to be returned to kitchen and become, like Clementine lost and gone forever.

It certainly was simple. It was perfect.

Ellie's point about the stolen car dissipated the small doubt that had developed with regard to Hogan's involvement but there was still no evidence. All that had been achieved, was the almost certain realisation that Hogan was the killer. However knowing that was not enough and the Director of Public Prosecutions would laugh them out of existence if all they had to present, was what they now had.

Harry knew this. He had already closed down the Cork inquiry, now he was about to do the same with the Limerick investigation. They might be pretty sure what had occurred after the drinks reception in the university but there was no way they were going to be able to connect Dennis Hogan to the killing of Miriam Nolan.

All that was left was Galway and they were having similar difficulties there. The probability was that Hogan had killed the Malone girl and although Dan had not fully exhausted his leads, the prognosis was not good.

It stuck in the experienced detective's craw that a man could get away with four killings and there was nothing that could be done. But there was worse, the beast was still in circulation and was still a danger to others. It was not outside the realms of possibility that another girl might die because of his inability to put Hogan away.

Harry could sense a feeling of despair and he knew that it was all that was left to motivate him to keep going, even if it were against all odds. There had been other cases, in other times, when Harry Tinto had faced the same predicament. It had not stopped him then. Neither would it stop him now.

9

Emer watched her friend across the restaurant table. She knew he was preoccupied. She was aware that this was a frustration he felt over the progress of the case. Harry did not like failure and liked even less the throwing in of the towel. He had told her of his thoughts as they had driven to Hunters Hotel in Ashford for a night out. She had suggested that getting personally involved in the case may not have been the wisest action to take. He agreed with her by saying that a policeman who gets personally involved is not acting in his own, the victim's or indeed the force's best interests. Harry then demolished his own argument by asking how a person cannot become involved, if failure might mean the death of another young woman.

However, a few glasses of wine and a good meal can do wonders for a melancholy man and the evening helped to lift Harry's spirits and steal his thoughts away from the case. It was a much needed interlude and as Emer was drinking as well, they conveniently decided to stay the night.

Emer awoke with a start to the sound of her mobile phone. It was five in the morning and the caller was her daughter, Nuala.

'Mum, is Harry with you?'

'Yes, he is.'

'Then get him to ring Sinead immediately, it's Fiona and the baby.'

Harry was awake by this time and within a minute was talking to his eldest daughter. He listened grimly.

'I'll be with you in forty five minutes.'

And he hung up.

Emer was already dressed and within minutes they were on the road. They had not stopped to discuss the emergency so it was only when they were driving that Harry gave Emer the details of what had happened. She had guessed most of it herself but Harry filled in the details. Fiona, it appeared, might have miscarried the baby and had been rushed to Holles Street maternity hospital. Sinead had not been sure of the exact details. She didn't know whether it was a risk of miscarriage or the real thing.

Harry raced through the dawn to be with his second child and her trouble. For once in his life, the law was expendable and he had no trouble with that. All his life he had known that, for him, there were only a few people above the law. All girls and all called Tinto.

At Holles Street Hospital, they were told that there hadn't been a miscarriage but that Fiona had suddenly gone into labour. She would be giving birth to a premature baby. Fiona was fine but they were not so sure about the baby. Sinead was with her and the doctors were doing everything they could.

The minutes seemed like hours and the hours felt like days as they waited. Just the two of them, sitting side by side. They didn't speak very much. There was no need for words. Companionship, at this time of anxiety, was all that was required.

It was nine fifteen and Harry and Emer saw Sinead walk towards them. She hadn't sighted them and her face betrayed no emotion. Suddenly she saw her father and with her beautiful face alight, she started running towards him and finally wrapped her arms around his neck and said.

'Dad, there's another female in the family to nag you.'

Tears welled up in Harry's eyes. All had ended well and as he gathered Emer and Sinead together he knew that life was good. At least it was for some people.

Sinead had been present at the birth and everything had gone well. The baby was small and might remain in hospital for an extra day or two but she was fine. The doctors had no anxieties about her.

Harry and Emer were allowed a few moments with Fiona but she was very tired.

'Dad, go and look at her, she's a beauty.'

Fiona smiled and was asleep.

Bending over her bed Harry kissed his sleeping daughter on the forehead.

A minute later as he looked at his little granddaughter for the first time, he felt a surge of love for the mite. Later, he remembered that there were other men who probably once felt these same emotions for four little girls, only to have their lives snuffed out by a wicked blade. There was nothing those men could do about it but he, Harry Tinto could.

Emer had asked a local officer to take their vehicle to Store Street some hours earlier, so they walked to the station. It had been a hectic few hours. Their evening had started with a tinge of despair, which turned to joy and passion, followed by the fear of tragedy and ending in great happiness.

Harry could feel it in himself. There was a spring in his step and he could sense a new beginning, not just in his family life but in his professional life as well. How long it would last he didn't know but he would drink from that chalice for as long as he could.

Harry let Dan and Ellie continue with their work in Galway. They were, as he calculated earlier, probably not going to achieve anything significant but it would be foolish to pull out before the investigation had run its course.

As for himself, the day had only started and it had been an extraordinary one so far. There had only been three others that had ever resembled it and those were the days when each of his own children had been born. They had all been different, yet all the same.

There were things to be done. Rita was probably still in her bed, blissfully unaware of the events of the previous hours. He would phone her with the good tidings of her elevation to the status of aunt.

Afterwards he would sneak back to Holles Street to gaze again at the little midget and to be at Fiona's side when she awoke. He knew that, for the foreseeable future, he would have two roles to play in the life of the baby. He would be both father and grandfather and he would relish both responsibilities greatly.

But as the day wore on, the fresh desire to bring justice to the four dead girls grew and Harry knew that Mark Dowd was to be his last best chance. It would end where it began, back in Bray with Joanne Boylan.

If he could persuade Dowd to give evidence about the night of the killing and the part that the minister had played in the death, then there could be a conviction and the streets would be safe from Dennis Hogan. But persuasion alone would not crack the nut. Harry needed some leverage that would encourage the solicitor to battle, as lawyers rarely do, in the interests of justice.

The legal profession flourished on the art of compromise, the ability to make the deal. The opportunity to mitigate retribution was the daily chore of the lawyer.

The opportunity, in this case, would need to provide some personal benefit to Dowd himself. Immunity from prosecution would appear to be the obvious carrot but Harry was unsure if that was available. Dowd had played no part in the killing but he was an accessory after the fact. So something else was needed.

Harry had postponed his interview with Dowd and had considered giving the solicitor a week to consider his position. After some reflection he had changed his mind, Harry would see him the next day. It was always better to strike while the iron was hot.

Dan McCarthy could see the writing on the wall as far as the investigation of Sarah Malone's death was concerned. There had been progress. It had almost certainly been established that Dennis Hogan was the killer but there was no proof. Nothing new had come to light that would form the basis of a criminal prosecution, so closing the book looked like the only realistic option available.

For Dan, there had been some consolation and that was meeting Ellie Kennedy. She was everything that he liked in a girl. Dan had been smitten immediately but had done nothing about it so far. But that was about to change.

It had been some day, a cocktail of the personal and the professional. Emer was happy for Harry that Fiona and her baby were fine and she was pleased that she had been part of it. She smiled when she thought of Nuala's phone call in the early hours. Both she and Sinead had taken the situation between their parents as the status quo and had thought no more about it. It seemed to her that both families had accepted their parents' relationship unreservedly. Yes, it had been a good day in more ways than one.

With Harry's mind temporarily diverted there was no new direction as to where the case was going. Billy and Pete knew that tomorrow would be different. The boss would be back in harness and Mark Dowd would be the subject of scrutiny in the impending interview. So the two men decided to leave the now empty incident room to its ghosts and go for a drink.

As they entered the lounge of the Great Northern, Billy stopped.

'Pete, I think we'll go somewhere else,' he said nodding in the direction of a young couple in an alcove at the far end of the room.

'Yes, I don't think they want our company,' Pete replied with a grin.

There was a pub just down the road and the two older gardaí would discreetly leave their younger colleagues to themselves.

'You know,' Billy remarked, 'first there was Harry and Emer and now these two. Store Street is becoming a right old dating service.'

And they both laughed.

Harry thought, as he gazed around the restaurant table in Temple Bar where six people were seated, that it was a strange celebration. There was Sinead and her husband Martin, Rita, Emer and her daughter Nuala as well as himself. However the people who were being celebrated were not present but were in safe hands, in Holles Street hospital. Harry had come directly from there.

Fiona and himself had talked. There had always been a bond between them but Harry had never felt it stronger and it felt good. The girls had been there earlier and the important task of finding a name for the baby had been discussed with all kinds of exotic and ordinary suggestions being made. It was when Fiona was alone with her father that she told him that she would like to give her baby her mother's name, if that was alright with him.

'Then Monica, she will be,' Harry replied.

Harry had not slept well that night. He could not rid himself of his thoughts about the case and in particular what enticement he could offer Dowd to give evidence for the state. It was a difficult issue and he felt a pressure to have the carrott available before the interview.

Eventually, at about three o'clock, he got up to make some tea. When this was ready he sat outside in his back garden. He felt a peace and a calm. There with no sound other than an occasional distant car to break the silence.

Dowd was a high flier and that did not happen by chance. He was a performer and he would figure that he could not be touched. Without a murder charge there mightn't be a charge of being an accessory and without Dowd's co-operation there could be no murder charge.

Then it came to him. The jacket. He had found a leverage. For the next hour the policeman remained in his garden, now that he had what he needed that might get Dowd onside, there were other things to think about.

However, if there was no breakthrough with the solicitor, Harry held out little hope of a successful conclusion to the case. Francis had been involved with Hogan all his professional life. Indeed, he was the beneficiary of many opportunities that were in the minister's gift. Francis was not going to bite the hand that had fed him all those years.

Dowd would be at the station around ten thirty. He had not liked the prospect of the interview being done at a police station but Harry had felt that official surroundings would concentrate the mind of the arrogant lawyer.

It was just after the appointed hour when they commenced. Billy was with Harry and Dowd was accompanied by his solicitor John Byrne. Byrne was known to Harry only by reputation. Harry had decided to permit Byrne to be present at the interview.

After the preliminary formalities, including the caution, Harry began addressing his remarks directly to Dowd.

'Thirty three years ago, a young girl was brutally murdered in an alley just off the sea front in Bray. Nobody has ever answered for that crime. I have re-opened the case and a new investigation into the killing has been in progress for some time. The genesis of this new inquiry was the death a few weeks ago of a school friend of yours, a Martin Devereaux.'

The detective paused for a moment, before continuing.

'You, Mark Dowd, have been seriously implicated in this killing and the purpose of this interview is to examine your involvement. We are aware and concede that your participation in the crime relates to the period of time directly before the girl died and the minutes and hours following her killing. I am aware that you played no part in the planning or perpetration of the slaying. What have you to say to these allegations?'

Dowd said nothing for a moment.

'Mr. Tinto, I have come here at your request on a voluntary basis, but I have nothing to say to your allegations and as I am not under arrest, I intend to terminate this interview and leave the station.'

He was finished.

Harry had not been surprised at the attitude that Dowd had taken. He hadn't expected any other response. However, the arrogance and the aggression of the response rolled off Harry.

'That may very well be what you are thinking of doing but should you follow that course of action, then a warrant will be issued for your arrest and you will be taken into custody. As a solicitor, you will be aware of the significant difference between helping me with my inquiries and being arrested.'

'You wouldn't dare,' Dowd hissed.

'It's your call,' Harry answered.

At this point John Byrne interjected.

'I would like a private word with my client,' he said.

Harry nodded and gestured to Billy to turn off the recorder and to withdraw.

John Byrne had done his homework. He knew who he was dealing with and his sources had warned him that Harry Tinto was a man to be reckoned with. His client's attitude and reaction would not help him in this situation.

'Look Mark,' Byrne said when the others had left the room, 'an outburst like you had there will get you nowhere with a guy like Tinto. You can't bully him, you can't intimidate him, you can't put him on the back foot. He's a superb policeman and even though he is in his late fifties he is still very much on top of his game. Bluster, status and a fine reputation counts for nothing. You can work with Tinto or against him. If you choose the latter, you lose.'

Dowd said nothing for a moment. He hadn't liked what he had just been told but Byrne was one of the best in the trade and his comments were not made lightly.

'I need some time for a re-think,' he finally said.

John Byrne left the room to see Harry.

He was back within a couple of minutes.

'Four o'clock, here tomorrow.' Byrne told his client.

The interview was over in less than fifteen minutes. Harry was pleased to agree to postpone the interview until the next day. The request for a postponement might signify that Dowd felt he needed to re-assess his situation. What had caused the change of heart he didn't know but he expected that a smart counsellor played a key role. Tomorrow, if experience was anything to go by, Dowd could present as a totally different interviewee.

An hour later in Byrne's rooms, Dowd told his solicitor the full story of the events that took place, so long ago. The principal elements of his tale were still clear but some of the detail had been obscured by time. When he was finished there was a pause for thought.

'I wonder what Tinto is after, what does he want?' Dowd asked.

'If your memory is accurate, Mark, then the worst possible scenario would be that you could be prosecuted as an accessory to murder. The question is whether that is likely? It's certainly a possibility but I don't think it is very likely. I think what Tinto wants is a witness to give evidence in a murder trial.'

'So where does that leave me?' Dowd asked.

'It all depends on what Tinto has. Firstly, to what extent are you implicated by Devereaux's statement? Secondly, what will Hutton say or what has he said? You say he's in hospital after suffering a stroke and is not at all well. The question is how well will he be in six month's or a year's time? Then there is Francis. Has Tinto interviewed him and if so what did he say?'

John Byrne stopped.

'Let's leave it for while, have a coffee and clear our minds.'

But over the coffee they continued.

'This is going to become public. It will ruin me both professionally and socially. It's not the money, I have all I'll ever need. It's the ignominy of serving time. My children would be disgraced and both Eileen and I would be ostracised by our social peers. All of that will happen, if I go on the witness stand and under oath admit to my involvement in the aftermath of a killing. I will, in effect, be convicting myself.'

'To some extent you're right, Mark but there are degrees of ruin and disgrace. I expect that in return for giving evidence it is possible that you might get a reduced custodial sentence. Your career as a top solicitor would be over. You might even escape disbarrment. All that would reduce the effect on your kids' lives to a period of embarrassment, but they should get over that quickly enough. As for the social effect on yourself and your wife, who can tell about that?'

It wasn't a palatable option as far as Dowd saw it. It was a fall from grace in a very public manner and a loss of those glittering prizes of celebrity and respect, admiration and status, things that mattered very much to him.

'But,' Byrne continued, 'that's just one option, there are other possibilities to examine. You can deny everything, you were never there and anyone who says you were is mistaken. That scenario is one that maybe you should give some thought to. Devereaux is dead and it is unlikely that anything he wrote could be used in a prosecution against you, so you can cross him off the list. He can't damage you. Then there is Michael Hutton, a stroke victim. It is by no means certain that he is going to make a credible witness. His mind may be fragile, his memory uncertain. That leaves Hogan and Francis and their close association makes it improbable that Tinto has got anything from them. You should co-operate fully with Tinto. You'll need to be patient with his questions. You mustn't show any aggression or annoyance but you must give him nothing.'

'That seems good to me,' Dowd interjected.

'Yes, but there may be a problem. We don't know what Tinto has and I think he has something incriminating. He is not the kind of man that goes off on a mystery tour.'

'So what do I do?'

'You take a middle route. You deny any involvement and if you persist with that strategy, Tinto will, sooner or later, have to show his hand. Then, if he has something damaging, you may have to come clean and accept the indignities that it will entail. The risk with this approach is that, if charged and found guilty, you will probably be given a more severe sentence.'

Dowd could follow John Byrne's strategy, but couldn't see what silver bullet the lawman could have. Dowd's confidence and self belief were returning and with it a touch of the old arrogance and he knew it. He would need to be careful. Dowd did not like the meek for they, in his opinion, never inherited anything. He would be very careful with Tinto. He needed to be because if Johnny Byrne considered him a formidable foe then he was a worthy opponent in this game of cat and mouse.

As Harry left Store Street he wondered if he should have released Dowd. He knew he was giving him the chance to marshal his thoughts and establish the position he would take. However Harry always took the long view and he was satisfied that his decision would eventually prove correct.

10

Later, as he walked down Merrion Square towards Holles Street hospital the case faded from Harry's mind, as he thrilled from the anticipation of seeing again his little granddaughter wriggling in her cot.

Fiona was well. She was alert and filled with awe at the prospect of motherhood and was surrounded, as Harry entered, by four women. There was Sinead and Rita, as well as Emer and Nuala and the hushed sounds of their conversation made Harry pause for a few moments before entering. He knew whatever happened to him in the future that his daughter and granddaughter would not be alone.

Harry and Billy did not know what to expect from Dowd at their afternoon meeting. Billy was a trifle optimistic but Harry knew that Dowd would not be an easy adversary. He was a man with a great deal of pride and self esteem and would not yield easily to the probes of the police.

Dowd, accompanied again by Johnny Byrne, was on time and all were soon installed for the interview process. The recordings were activated and the formalities and cautions observed before Harry commenced questioning.

'Mr Dowd, tell me what you can about the night of July 10th 1977?' Harry asked.

'That's more than thirty years ago, I have no recollection of that day whatsoever.'

'My information suggests that on that night, in Bray, you participated in the disposal of the body of Joanne Boylan.'

'I have never heard of a Joanne Boylan and have never been party to any criminal activity, let alone a killing,' Dowd answered.

There was an ease and confidence to his response that suggested that he felt that he was in the clear, that he was untouchable and that the detective had nothing that he could pin on him.

Harry was not surprised and was ready.

'Mr Dowd, as you have been told, we are investigating the death of Joanne Boylan. What you are not aware of is that there are three other murder investigations being carried out in conjunction with her killing. It has been confirmed that all the killings were perpetrated by the same person. The other young girls who died were killed in very similar circumstances. As far as I am concerned anybody who protected Joanne's killer is morally responsible, to some degree, for the deaths of three other girls. If they had not given refuge to a murderer, three women would be alive today.'

Harry stopped to allow his words sink in. Dowd said nothing. His face showed no reaction. It was the eyes that betrayed him. A quick glance in his solicitor's direction was enough to tell the detective that Dowd was shaken but that was not the same as being broken and Harry Tinto was very conscious of that.

'I ask you again Mr. Dowd where were you on the night of July 10th 1977?'

'As I told you, it's so long ago that I have no idea.' Dowd responded.

There was silence.

'Our information suggests a different story,' Harry said.

'Well, I don't know what you have been told or by whom but I assure you that I have told you the truth.'

Another pause and Harry knew that this could be kept going all day with no results. He would go directly to the nub of the matter.

'I am aware of the game you are playing, Mr Dowd. You believe that you have certain options open to you. The problem is that any of them could have a catastrophic effect on your life. Your attitude today suggests that you are withholding information that protects a man who killed on at least four occasions. There is no reason to believe that if this man is placed in the same or similar circumstances in the future, that he will not kill again. Your self interest may be endangering the life of some young woman as we speak. If that attitude persists, you can expect no breaks from me.'

Harry watched Dowd and his solicitor, both of whom shifted uncomfortably in their seats.

'Dowd, I expect that you have been advised that there is little chance of you being charged as an accessory to murder, if the killer has not been charged and found guilty. You may ask what evidence there is? You've been advised to play it cool and not to get ruffled, answer my questions, don't rock the boat and remember that you have not been arrested, you are just helping the authorities with their inquiries.'

Harry continued.

'But advice given and followed when the full facts are not available can have a disastrous impact on your future.'

Harry stood up suddenly.

'I wish to consult with my colleague for a few minutes,' he said and motioned to Billy to join him outside.

'Time for a coffee, Billy,' he said when the door of the interview room closed behind them.

'We'll let them think about what has transpired, for a while.'

Once they were alone Dowd turned to his solicitor.

'I think we have him on the run, Johnny.'

'Don't be foolish, you've seen the police interview clients as many times as I have. They don't operate like this man. There is none of the constantly repeated questions over several hours. No, this guy is different and I think he has something. I wouldn't be surprised if he has the case against Hogan all but sown up and what he wants is for you to make it airtight.'

'If that's the case where do I stand?'

'I think that he will destroy you if you don't give him what he wants.'

Dowd was immediately struck by how quickly things had changed. Only moments ago he was full of confidence that events were going his way. Now he was under pressure and could feel the perspiration begin to moisten his hands.

'Why? Why would he take that attitude?'

Byrne took a minute to answer.

'Because, by your answers to his questions, you have stated that you are prepared to put some woman's life in jeopardy in order to avoid facing the consequences of your own actions?'

'So, what's next?' Dowd asked.

'We can stick with our strategy, admit nothing, give him nothing and see what he pulls out of the bag. I'd wager that there is something in that bag.'

The door opened and Billy entered followed moments later by the Superintendent. The recording was re-activated and Harry restarted the interview.

'Right, Mr. Dowd do you persist with your position that you were not involved in the death of Joanne Boylan.'

With a quick glance in Byrne's direction he answered.

'I have not changed my position. I have told you the truth.'

'Now, Mr. Dowd let me tell you something. Everybody makes a mistake and Joanne Boylan's killer made a mistake. Of course, it wasn't a mistake then but it is now. You may wonder how that can be. Well the answer is simple. DNA analysis has been developed in the intervening years. DNA does not deteriorate very much over thirty years. We have the jacket. Now, if you weren't there, you won't remember this but a man's jacket was thrown over the girl's face. You will no doubt be pleased to learn that the jacket was in perfect condition when retrieved. You will, I'm sure, excuse me again as I want to bring in a forensic technician to take a swab from you for DNA analysis. With you permission, of course.'

The effect of this was electric. Dowd was frozen, speechless. The colour drained from his face. He could hardly turn to face his counsellor.

'I need a few minutes,' John Byrne said to Harry.

The Superintendent agreed and both detectives left for a second time.

It took minutes before Dowd recovered his composure and was ready to talk to his solicitor. Byrne had warned him that he expected Tinto to have something up his sleeve, but he never expected it to be the jacket. What had caused his shock was the fact that the possible existence of the garment had never crossed his mind in all the years since that fateful night and the remembrance that he had worn Hogan's jacket for a while that night. He didn't know whether he could have left DNA on it, he didn't know enough about this new technology. DNA could provide absolute proof that he had been in contact with the girl. It was only a small additional step to show that he had participated in her death.

Dowd knew the game was over. He was in it now, up to his neck and he needed to be upfront about everything. There could be no holding back, no slanting, no attempts to minimise his involvement. The need was to concentrate his efforts on minimising the effect of this on his family. Damage limitation was now the only game in town.

When Harry and Billy came back in, they knew that a battle had been won but one victory didn't win the war. However, it was a start. By the end of the day they would have a signed statement from the solicitor describing what had happened on that July night. Harry was confident that Dowd would hold nothing back this time, so he gave him time to think and prepare for making the statement.

A brisk walk, a coffee and a sandwich would replenish him for the afternoon, which would be long on detail and short on excitement. But the plan did not materialise as Harry's feet took on a life and will of their own, taking the detective from Store Street to Merrion Square, to Holles Street hospital, to a baby in a cot.

Later, Harry listened to what Mark Dowd had to say. The evening he described was typical of any group of young students. There were drinks and conversation, with the latter turning to discussion first and later to argument. It was not argument in the public order sense but what the students would consider debate.

There were eight people present in the group. The names were the same as before, Devereaux and Hutton, Hogan and Francis, then the three lads that Hutton had mentioned, Doyle, Jones and Canavan. There was, of course, himself.

Dowd's description of the topics debated matched what Michael Hutton had told Harry. Then, at closing time, they moved on to a disco. The solicitor described the group as having had a good deal to drink, but nobody had been out of their mind.

He couldn't remember much about the disco. They had planned to meet up again afterwards unless, of course, they had met someone.

The disco had finished about three o'clock and a few of them met outside afterwards. Doyle, Canavan and Jones had gone their separate ways.

Hogan was animated and told the others he had something to show them and without much coaxing Devereaux, Hutton, Francis and himself had gone with him to see what he was talking about.

At this point Dowd took a break and Harry had a question.

'Am I correct in understanding that when you were leaving the vicinity of the disco you didn't know what you were going to see?'

'That is correct. Well, at least, I didn't know what we were going to be shown. I would swear it was the same for all the others.'

Dowd continued.

'Hogan opened the boot of a car when we got there and we saw the body instantly. The girl was lying face upwards. I knew who she was and so did the others. I can remember being too stunned to say anything, too shocked to think.'

'Did anyone say anything about how this situation came about or admit to the killing?' Harry asked.

'Hogan was very excited. I don't remember him admitting anything but I presumed that he was the killer.'

Dowd stopped talking.

'What was your condition at this point?' Harry asked.

'We had been drinking continuously for more that five hours. We weren't legless but we were certainly intoxicated. The sensible, responsible reaction would have been to have gone to the police but we didn't do that.'

'Why not?'

'I'll never know but it was probably a combination of the alcohol and selfishness.'

'Selfishness what do mean by that?' the detective prompted.

'I suppose the fact that we were at the scene and had been drinking where the girl worked. We had discussed subjects like a perfect crime. Our judgement had been warped into believing that we were involved. I was a law student at the time. Being involved in a murder would have been disastrous for my career. Foolishly, I chose to help conceal the crime.'

Dowd looked around the room for a moment.

'I never, in my wildest nightmares, thought that thirty years later I would end up being interviewed about the episode.'

'What happened next?' Harry asked.

'We were in shock. I can't remember being outraged. Then someone suggested we dump the body in the mountains. Who that was I have no recollection, but it could have been any one of us. Francis went with Hogan in the stolen car with the body. I presumed Hogan had stolen it. Devereaux had his mother's car and he, Hutton and I followed them up towards Roundwood where we dumped the body.'

'Did Hogan offer any explanation as to what had occurred?'

'Only what he said when he pointed to the car boot. Look what I have found.'

There was silence for a time before Dowd continued.

'Dev, Hutton and I met the next day to discuss what we might do but the remains had been discovered and we believed there wasn't anything to be gained by going to the authorities. So we did nothing. It's amazing how naïve young people can be.'

Dowd had finished his story but Tinto still had some questions. However they all needed a breather so Harry decided to take a break for an hour.'

'Well Billy, what do you think about that?' Harry asked as they left the station for a coffee.

'It's not exactly what was said in the letter.'

'And it's not exactly the same as Hutton's version either. Dowd didn't hear any admission of guilt. I had been relying on him to confirm Hutton's statement to me that Hogan had admitted doing the killing. Devereaux's letter placed the responsibility at Hogan's door alone, as well.'

Later Harry got back to the interview with Dowd. Billy had gone on his way, so he had Pete join him. For three hours they trawled through the solicitor's memories in search of some detail that would give them a handle on the events of that night.

As matters stood, nothing very much had changed. Hogan was still the suspect, not just for the death of Joanne Boylan but for the other young girls as well. He still had the opportunity and the psychological motivation for the killings was still valid.

Harry needed some time to ponder the ramifications of Dowd's statement. If there were some serious discrepancies in the recollections of his three witnesses where did that leave him? Whose remembrance was the most reliable? Harry had little difficulty coming to an informed answer on that question.

Mark Dowd's training and experience was all about the attention to detail and even though he was just a student lawyer at the time of the killing, the importance of detail would already be part of his nature. Devereaux's contribution would be the least reliable. His letter was the final act of a man on a journey of self destruction. It was unsigned and this would make it inadmissible in court. Harry would like to talk to Hutton again but whether that would come to pass was anybody's guess at this point.

It had taken several hours to get Dowd's statement completed. Emer had typed it out and then it had been vetted by John Byrne and signed by Mark Dowd.

It was late when Harry and Emer caught up with Fiona in Holles Street hospital but she had not been alone, Sinead and Rita had spent the evening with her.

Two days into motherhood and Fiona was ready for a lifelong commitment. She would remain in hospital for another day. There was good news. Little Monica would be going home with her mother the next day. The news of this startled the policeman, a kind of panic set in. What was he to do? Nothing was ready.

Harry was told not to worry, everything was okay. All matters would be looked after. The women in his life, who now numbered five, had everything organised.

Much later, Harry remarked to Emer, as they drove home, how much life had changed for him in just a short space of time. He had his surgery and his recovery had been complete. He had met her and had been seriously and terminally smitten. His eldest daughter had married, so now he had a son-in-law. And then there was little Monica. He really was a fortunate man.

11

The morning began with Harry briefing the team on the previous evening's events. They were, of course, aware of the interview with Dowd but not the detail of what had been admitted.

Harry had asked Billy to get a background profile of Peter Francis. This was now ready.

'What do we know about Francis? He went to school in St. Dominick's College then proceeded to university in Belfield. There, he studied Business and graduated with a modest degree. He went, almost immediately, into the property business and remained there for fourteen years. Around the same time as Hogan first got elected to the Dáil, Peter Francis changed career direction and moved into public relations. He was good at it. After a few years he had established his own firm and enjoyed a considerable amount of success. He was well liked and had a reputation for being reliable. He was earning a good living but nothing spectacular. Then his old friend, Hogan, was appointed a government minister and Francis got a PR contract for his department. Very quickly, Francis was working almost exclusively for Hogan. They have been together ever since.

Harry walked down the quays. He was enjoying the autumn sunshine and at the same time examining the elements of his investigation. He drew no comfort from his conclusions. He doubted that there was sufficent evidence to get a murder conviction.

There were aspects of the investigation that Harry now needed to consider. Before his interview with Dowd he had closed down their investigations in Cork and Limerick. He expected that he would be doing the same in Galway shortly. But now was not the time to make the decision. It would be sufficient to do so if and when his two detectives had finished their inquiries.

Emer knew that everything could soon come to a halt. She could not see where any conclusive evidence would come from that would be sufficient to convict Hogan. Hutton, although slightly improved, was incapable of giving reliable evidence in a court of law. Dowd's testimony, which was reliable, couldn't identify the killer of Joanne Boylan. Hogan's defence would use this testimony to show reasonable doubt.

Harry wondered whether Hogan and Francis were expecting a visit and whether they had discussed a strategy? Speculating was useless and would only encourage him to make assumptions which might not be helpful.

The first step would be to decide who to interview first. It probably didn't matter but he felt that the balance favoured starting with the minister. It would be an unprecedented step. It was almost certainly the first occasion on which a government minister was interviewed by the gardaí in connection with a murder.

Harry knew he had to be careful and not just for his own sake. He knew he was untouchable as long as he remained professional. However, there was a serious doubt that there was sufficent evidence to convict Hogan of any of the killings. To put his suspicions into the public domain would be unacceptable. The papers, particularly the tabloids, would go after Hogan and the politician would be damaged beyond repair by their antics. The constitutional position was that a man was innocent until proven guilty.

It was also Tinto's law.

It had been a little tricky getting into direct contact with Dennis Hogan. Harry didn't want to march into the department and demand to see the minister. That would be one sure way of getting the tongues to wag.

A circuitous route was needed and Harry went to the top. He went to Matt Dolan.

Within an hour, Hogan had contacted Harry. All Dolan had done was to inform the minister that a detective needed to talk to him and wanted to be discreet.

After he had replaced the handset, Harry pondered the call. It had been brief and business like. No hint had been given that the minister was troubled by the request or the interest the detective had shown in keeping the matter under wraps. This was not the reaction the detective would normally expect and it suggested to Harry that there could have been an element of rehearsal in it. The response was one that could not be drummed up in a matter of minutes. No, Hogan was expecting the contact and was prepared. That was something worth knowing, Harry thought.

'Billy, work on your own for a few days, go over everything again and if something hits you, follow your instinct. There is no need to report, just let me know if you find anything interesting.'

As he drove home he knew that the next morning would be trying and he knew he needed to be master of his craft for his session with Dennis Hogan. But the evening was his and it was to be memorable.

Sinead and Rita were taking Fiona and little Monica home. It would be another night of celebration, albeit this time it would be quiet. Although, he expected the pair to be tired he wanted to have a few words with Fiona alone.

As he entered his cul de sac he could see his home and it looked deserted. There were a few cars parked outside his gate. There was Emer's, Sinead's and the third belonged to Martin and they sent bells ringing. Another vehicle would now be needed.

Inside the house, the sounds were muted and he guessed that a certain little mite had a big day and was, for now, asleep. He was right. The adults were talking in whispers, eating Chinese takeaways and drinking wine. Harry Tinto joined his family.

Billy had got to work immediately and, in his methodical way, started at the beginning with the death of Joanne Boylan.

Thirty three years was a very long time but it was not a lifetime. Nobody in Bray had remembered the case but there must have been some officers, who had worked the case all those years ago, still alive. It would take some doing, but it might be worth tracking them down.

So he went directly into the old documents of the case to generate a list of gardaí who had been involved in the investigation. Once that was completed he could start his search for them. Some of them, he was certain, would have died but others would be fit and alert and who knows maybe that nugget that Harry needed might come from them.

It was after eleven o'clock and Harry was alone with Fiona in the kitchen. They both had something to say and it was Fiona who spoke first.

She needed to tell her father how she felt about all that had been done for her and her little girl and how she was sorry that she was now going to be a burden on him. His way of life and his quiet peaceful home would now become a place filled with sound and fury. And suddenly there were tears. But they were tears of hope and joy, of love and happiness.

Harry put his arms around his second daughter and allowed her time for her tears and later as they both drank coffee around the kitchen table he told her what she needed and what he wanted. His wish was that his granddaughter would want for nothing. Monica would have everything that any other infant would have.

'There is something you're going to need, Fiona. You are going to need a car to get the two of you around. I won't have Monica on the back of a bike.'

They both laughed at that and for Fiona, there were some more tears.

Dennis Hogan had wanted to meet at his Ballsbridge apartment but Harry rejected that. They had finally compromised by agreeing to meet in Hogan's solicitor's rooms in the suburban village of Blackrock.

Harry had decided to take Emer with him. He was not going to allow Hogan to believe that they were just going through the motions. The interview would be on a par with what would be likely to occur if the interview was taking place in official surroundings.

The time had been arranged for ten o'clock and all parties were there. Hogan's solicitor made the introductions but there was no camaraderie. Harry had felt, after the phone call the previous day, that Hogan had been expecting a visit from the police. His body language this morning was sending signals of irritation and annoyance, that a man of his importance was being subjected to this nonsense.

Before the interview got underway, Maurice Brown, Hogan's solicitor spoke.

'Mr. Tinto, I don't believe there is any necessity to have these proceedings recorded.'

'On the contrary, it is my view that it is essential.' Harry replied.

'My client feels that your attitude to this...'

Harry interjected.

'What your client feels is of little importance to me but if he wishes for this interview to take place in Store Street then I'll have no difficulty obliging him.'

Brown saw immediately that Harry was serious and withdrew.

'Well then, are we ready to proceed?'

Both men facing him nodded their assent.

Harry began with the official caution and as he did so he noticed a slight drop in the minister's face. It was as if, for the first time, Hogan realised that this was a serious business.

'Mr Hogan, you are not under arrest at this point and you don't have the right to have your legal counsellor with you but for the moment I am permitting you this privilege. This interview concerns an investigation into the murder of Joanna Boylan in Bray in July of 1977. There are other killings, which we believe to be related, under review, as well. We believe that you were involved in the death of Joanne Boylan.'

Harry paused briefly.

'Mr. Hogan, could you tell me what happened on the night of July 10th 1977 in the bar of the International Hotel?'

Hogan said nothing. He had clearly not being expecting this blunt question and turning to Brown asked.

'Do I need to answer this man's questions?' he asked as he got to his feet.

'No, you don't.'

'Then get me out of here.' The politician yelled.

'Calm down, Dennis, calm down.' His solicitor urged.

The minister stopped, he knew he had blown it and he sat down.

It was now Maurice Brown's turn.

'Should my client refuse to answer your questions and leave here, what will you do next?'

'Should Mr. Hogan decide on that course of action, I will immediately arrest him. He will be taken into custody and taken to Store Street station by squad car for questioning about the death of Joanne Boylan and other deaths.' Harry replied.

'Could I have some time with my client?' Brown asked.

'Sergeant Ryan and I will go for a coffee, we'll be about thirty minutes.' Harry answered.

'Thank you, Superintendant.'

Just down the street from Brown's rooms there was a sad café but it would do, coffee was coffee anywhere.

'That outburst was unexpected. It indicates a lack of control, anger and being taken by surprise. It may be the reaction of an innocent man but Hogan is not innocent.' Harry said.

'Another thing Harry, he is a politician and they are not the meek of the land. They have strong personalities. They are tough and they want to be in control. I think it's possible that Hogan was trying to sell us an act.'

'You may very well be right. But why would he do that? Later when he knows more of what information we have there might be some point. Anyway it won't work.'

Billy had worked late the previous evening compiling the names of all the gardaí involved in the original investigation. He had ended up with a list of twenty four names. Billy had half expected that there might be a few familiar names from a distant time among the pack but there were none. Harry and Joyce, he knew, had been stationed in Bray at the time and they might be able to help him locate or eliminate some of his two dozen names.

Billy would go to the boss.

Other officers wouldn't consider doing this. They would wait until their immediate superior was available but not Billy. As far as he was concerned Donal Joyce was a garda first and a Chief Superintendent second.

Billy's request for a few minutes both surprised and pleased Donal Joyce. He knew Billy of old and was aware of the scrapes, rows and discipline difficulties that had loomed large throughout his career. Joyce also knew that Billy was a good cop, maybe even an exceptional one. It was regrettable that Lynch's personality clashes had blighted his career. Joyce was also aware that Billy had been side stepped into, what might have been considered, sheltered employment by Harry Tinto. Harry would get the best out of him. There would be no rows. Billy would retire honourably.

'I will only take two minutes of your time, Sir.' Billy said as his head appeared around the door.

Joyce motioned for him to come and be seated and Billy duly obliged.

'This is a list of officers who were serving in Bray at the time of the Boylan killing,' Billy said, 'would you know the whereabouts of any of them?'

Joyce looked down the list carefully and taking his ballpoint he crossed off five names.

'These five, I know are deceased, there could be others. Johnny Doyle lives in Drumcondra and Jack Lyons is now a resident in the Blue Haven retirement home in Bray. The others I don't know but I doubt if many of them are still serving in the force.'

And that was all. Joyce, for a moment, had toyed with the idea of asking how the case was progressing but had thought better of it. Billy Lynch would have told him nothing. It would be Billy's view that if the Chief Superintendent wanted a progress report he could ask Tinto.

As he returned to the office, Billy decided to enlist the assistance of Ellie Kennedy to help him track down the whereabouts of the remaining officers. The young garda was efficient and obliging. Billy liked the girl.

Harry and Emer did not delay. They had given Brown enough time to get his client sorted out, if that was what he needed.

When facing Hogan across the table again, Harry decided to continue as before.

'Mr. Hogan, can you tell me of your whereabouts on July 10th 1977?'

'That's a long time ago Superintendent, I have no idea what I was doing that day.'

'Let me help you. It was the night that Joanne Boylan was stabbed to death in a cul de sac in Bray.'

'I'm afraid that means nothing to me. I don't know the girl and her name rings no bells for me.'

These initial exchanges told Harry that Hogan was going to deny everything. He was going to try and brazen it out. He had nothing to lose by taking that approach and he probably felt that he could extricate himself from the mess. He was wrong.

'Mr. Hogan,' Harry continued, 'are you acquainted with Martin Devereaux?'

'Yes, I knew Martin. He was a friend from my schooldays, he died recently.'

'Before your friend killed himself he left a statement implicating you in the girl's death.'

'Well, he was mistaken, I had nothing to do with that girl's death. Perhaps it was his illness that confused him. Besides his state of mind, just prior to taking his own life, must be questionable.'

'But he is not the only one. Michael Hutton and Mark Dowd, have said much the same as Devereaux,' Harry told him.

'Let me repeat Superintendent, I had nothing to do with the girl's death. I didn't know her and I know nothing at all about the incident. Are you finished?'

'Not at all Mr. Hogan, there is a lot more.'

Harry shuffled through the papers in front of him, then looking towards, Emer, he whispered 'Cork'.

The garda rooted through the files on the chair beside her, picked one and handed it to her boss. It was a strategy they had arranged prior to the interview. The purpose of it was to allow for a little time, when nothing was happening. It could, in some people, have the effect of making them anxious, putting them on the back foot. It also gave Harry a few moments to think.

'Mr. Hogan, does the name Angela Forde mean anything to you?'

'I can't say that it does. Should it?'

'Can you give me an account of your movements for the evening of April 21st 1982?'

'That's almost thirty years ago. I don't see how I can be expected to remember one particular night so long ago.'

'Let me help you. It was the night of the Gala dinner at the annual auctioneers' conference in Cork. You were there?'

Hogan hesitated for a moment. There was now less aggression in his demeanour. Then he answered haltingly.

'Yes, I was there.'

'We know you attended the dinner. You signed a menu for another delegate. We have the card. Did you meet Angela Forde?'

'I don't know who you are talking about. What has all this got to do with me?'

'Angela was a student, she worked part time as a waitress. She served at the function that you attended. Later, she was killed in an identical manner to the way that Joanne Boylan died. A pathologist has indicated that it is a near certainty that both girls were killed by the same individual. '

The government minister said nothing.

'Mr. Hogan, I ask you again. Did you kill Angela Forde?

'No, I did not,' he shouted in reply.

'Can you cast your mind back to the period after you had been demoted to the back benches?'

The minister nodded.

'On February the fourth, the year was....'

'1999.' Hogan interjected.

'You were in Galway opening a fitness centre and afterwards you spent time with the local cumann members. This was, it has been suggested, with a view to ascertaining how much support you had in the western constituency, as a national politician. Later that evening you attended a dinner in the Ardilaun hotel. Do you remember meeting Sarah Malone?'

Hogan did not answer immediately. The aggression had disappeared from his face, now turmoil was clearly visible.

'Yes, I met Sarah. She died too.'

Harry said nothing, allowing the pause to encourage Hogan to continue.

'I knew her father well, he supported me. I was at the funeral. Was she killed in the same way and by the same person as the others?' he asked.

'Did you kill Sarah Malone?' Harry asked.

'No, I did not kill Sarah.' Hogan replied vehemently.

'It is a matter of public record that you were a guest at an economics symposium in the University of Limerick on the evening of November 9th. 2005. Our information is that afterwards you attended a drinks reception. On that occasion did you meet a student called Miriam Nolan?'

121

'I have no recollection of the occasion or of meeting a Miriam Nolan but if I was there, and I don't question your information, I suppose I could have met the girl. However, I don't remember the event.'

The answer was reasonable. It would be impossible for a politician to recall every meeting he attended and everyone he was introduced to.

'On that night, the girl was killed in an identical fashion to the other three. Did you kill Miriam Nolan, Minister?' Harry asked slowly.

'No, I did not.' Hogan answered decisively.

'Mr. Hogan, we have four young women dead over a thirty year period of time, all, according to an expert, killed in the same way and almost certainly by the same person. We can place you close to the scene of all four killings. To put that down to coincidence would, I believe, be very foolish. Things don't happen that way.'

Harry stopped for a moment and then continued.

'Have you anything further to say?'

'All this has nothing to do with me,' the politician replied.

'I am not ready as this point to prefer a charge but I will want to speak to you again. Cancel your meeting in Brussels and don't leave the jurisdiction.'

Hogan said nothing

'One last thing, Mr. Hogan, you will be watched. I don't want another young girl slashed to death.'

Harry got up to leave and Emer terminated the recording. There was silence on the other side of the table.

It was clear that Maurice Brown was overwhelmed by the enormity of what he had just heard.

Hogan knew that should any of what had just been said enter the public domain his career in politics would be over. It would be splashed across the tabloids for days, maybe weeks. It would destroy him. And there was nothing he could do. It would be a time for calm and thought, where analysis and good judgement were needed.

Billy liked Ellie and the younger garda returned a respect that Lynch had rarely encountered during his police career and he appreciated the gift. So, for one of the few times in all his years in the force, Billy Lynch was comfortable working with someone else.

122

The two had made progress with the list of gardaí serving in Bray at the time of the killing that Billy had extracted from the files. After Joyce's seven names had been taken into account there remained seventeen officers to be accounted for. The human resources department of the force had provided what was needed. Five more on the list were deceased, nine had retired and three were still in the service.

The grand total was fourteen and Billy would need to talk to them and he wanted young Kennedy with him. However that would be up to Harry. He would ask Ellie to prioritise them on the basis of rank at the time of the killing. He reasoned that the higher the rank the more informatiom they would be able to provide. It also crossed Billy's mind that the higher the rank the older the officer and the greater the chance of forgetfulness. He didn't dwell on this.

'I don't know how much good we did there.' Harry said to Emer as they returned from the interview. 'If he is guilty, we will certainly have worried him. The different killings will have been linked and no killer can ever be certain that he didn't make a mistake. Hogan will probably assume that if we know about the other deaths that we also have something decisive to link him to one or more of the killings.'

'Which, of course, we don't have,' Emer added.

'That's right,' Harry said thoughtfully.

The jacket. Its perceived existence after all the years had shaken Dowd. Perhaps the tactic could be used another time. Harry wondered what happened to it. It must be somewhere. It would seem, to Harry, unlikely that it would have been disposed of even after thirty years.

This was where Billy might be able to help. Billy had phoned early in the afternoon and told Harry of his intention to track down all the officers from the Bray station. He had said that most of them were still living and he would be checking to see what they might remember. Harry asked Billy to check if any of them recalled anything about the jacket. It was a long shot, a very long shot but one never knew.

Harry was surprised when he got back to Store Street. Billy was waiting for him and had a request. It was this request that gave the Superintendent the shock of his professional life. Billy Lynch was looking for a partner.

Harry had no hesitation assigning Ellie Kennedy to Lynch for the few days. Together they would get through the remaining names quicker.

Ellie, Harry thought, had no idea what she was letting herself in for. If she had any plans for the next forty eight hours she could forget about them.

The team, apart from Billy and Ellie, assembled after lunch and listened to Emer's recording of the interview with Hogan. The minister had given nothing away and even his early outburst, when transferred to paper, would appear innocuous. Of course, only Harry and Emer had seen the facial expressions and the body language. The truth was that neither of them could be sure that the celebrated man they were interviewing was guilty of a killing or innocent of murder. If the interview had taken place in Store Street the video would have caught it all.

The next step would be Peter Francis. Arrangements would be made to interview him the following day. There wouldn't be any need, this time, for same level of discretion, although Harry recognised that until there was a charge, the individual's good name needed to be protected from a circulation chasing press.

On this occasion he would take either Dan or Pete with him. Harry had noticed in the last few days that Pete had been less visible than usual. He worked quietly at his desk. He was present in the incident room but was contributing very little and Harry wondered whether he was alright but he wouldn't ask. Everyone needs privacy from time to time. Everybody has problems and sometimes these demons needed to be addressed by the individuals themselves and frequently are not helped by even the best intentioned inquiry.

Ellie Kennedy was enjoying her new role. She had heard tales of Billy Lynch from colleagues outside the investigation. These were stories of a loner, a maverick, a man who was difficult to work with. The anecdotes were apparently legion but Ellie found no evidence of any of this.

They had commenced their interviews and were moving quickly through the list. Billy told her that this was not good because the speedier the job was, the less productive the work.

Nothing of any value had surfaced so far. Most had forgotten the details of the investigation while remembering the horror of the crime. Nobody recalled what had happened to the jacket. Everybody presumed it had been kept with the other evidence. But it was early days yet and they only needed one breakthrough. They would soldier on.

It was clear to Harry that Galway would produce nothing that would lead to a conviction. He closed the case of Sarah Malone just as he done with the Angela Forde and Miriam Nolan cases. If there was to be any success it would be with Joanne Boylan but even that looked uncertain at this time.

Harry Tinto did not know very much about DNA. He didn't really understand the science and was dubious that DNA would remain on a garment for thirty four years. However, his inquiries had assured him that the passage of time need not affect the DNA presence on the jacket, provided that the article had been stored carefully.

Emer was thoughtful. Different events were pulling Harry in all directions. There was the stress of the work and the dispiriting effects of the lack of progress. Then there was Fiona and little Monica. His granddaughter had given the man a new lease of life but Emer had not forgotten that it was still only six months since his cardiac surgery and he still needed to be careful. Harry had forgotten that he was still recovering. He was, she knew, still taking his medication but the exercise, that he had been told to take, was beginning to fall by the wayside. The girls, in the euphoria of the new arrival, saw their dad as the invincible hero he had always been and not the slightly wounded man, he had become. The present regime could not continue unabated. Something needed to be done.

Emer knew this did not involve huge adjustments. Fiona's situation would settle down into a routine very quickly and the case would slow down and terminate one way or another in the next week or so. But Harry needed to be back in a way of life that suited his situation. A few days away from the hurly burly of it all, might be a tonic and it would give them a chance to think of other things.

Harry had been correct with his assessment of Pete Halpin's demeanour. Pete was not well. His doctor had confirmed that tests had shown that he had prostate cancer. He had not been surprised. He had experienced most of the symptoms associated with the condition. Pete had read up on the condition prior to the tests and was aware of the different strains of the illness. The medics had assured him that he had contracted one of the milder versions of the condition and that he would be fine, at least in the short term. As for the long haul, who could say?

Harry felt that the interview in the morning could be one of the last. After it, they had nowhere else to go. He didn't expect that Francis would provide him with much.

Over a pint on his way home, Harry got a concerned earful from Emer. He was overdoing it. He couldn't argue with her. He was pleased that she had taken the initiative again and had arranged another weekend away. She had even looked after his domestic arrangements, organising her daughter, Nuala to stay with Fiona and Rita. If the truth were told he was feeling a little tired by all the activity. He needed the rest.

The interview with Peter Francis was arranged to take place in Store Street and no concessions had been granted. The interview would take place without the presence of Francis's legal advisor.

Pete had told Harry of his medical issue the previous evening so he had taken Dan into the interview with him.

After the recording was activated Harry began by formally cautioning Francis, who appeared unconcerned by the whole rigmarole. It wasn't clear whether this attitude stemmed from his ignorance of the seriousness of the situation he was in or whether it was just arrogance.

When Harry asked him about the events of the night of Joanne Boylan's death, he denied any involvement in the death and disposal of the girl's remains. He knew nothing of what had happened to the girl. He could have been drinking in the International Hotel with the others on the night in question but he had no memory of the night and that was all.

Harry pushed but to no avail.

He had been, he said, to the University of Limerick on several occasions over the years. Whether he was there on November 9th 2005 he couldn't say but at the time he was a PR advisor to the minister so Harry could check with the department.

It was useless. Nothing of any value was gleaned from the interview and Harry felt frustration rising within him. The investigation was in a cul de sac, a dead end. There appeared to be nowhere else to go.

Francis had denied very little. He said he had no knowledge of the Boylan killing. Yet, he accepted that he could have been in Bray at the time. How could he know where he was at a particular time three decades later? He had incriminated nobody. He had performed well and Harry wondered whether he had been coached. There were only two candidates for the job, Hogan and Dowd and the betting was on the former.

They would leave everything for the weekend. Everybody needed some rest and relaxation, not least himself. They would re-assess everything on the Monday.

12

Dan was pleased with the weekend break. There was an exhibition match followed by a celebratory dinner and a dance. At this point he did not have a date although his celebrity would ensure that he would not be alone. But Dan had an idea of his own. Maybe Ellie...... . At least, he could always ask.

Billy plans for the weekend did not include much rest and relaxation. A meal out and a few drinks for himself and his wife on the Friday night and Croke Park on the Sunday afternoon would be the height of it.

There was some burrowing to be done on the Saturday. Billy did not expect Ellie to interrupt her weekend plans for a few further interviews. Ellie Kennedy did not see it that way. She had no commitments on the Saturday morning.

The two gardaí had no difficulty finding the Blue Haven retirement home in Bray and Jack Lyons was in fine fettle when they met him. Jack, Billy had reckoned, must now be in his late seventies and although confined to a wheel chair his intellectual faculties were clear and sharp. Mr. Dementia had not paid this man a visit.

Jack Lyons was delighted to see them, he had few callers. His wife had passed on some years before and all the family that remained were some nephews. Jack Lyons was almost a forgotten man.

The old man remembered the Boylan case vividly. There was no need to remind him of the details. They were as fresh in his mind as if the crime had been committed recently.

At the time he had been a sergeant and was actively involved in the investigation. He recalled how the inquiry had come to an abrupt end. There had been no leads to follow.

'I remember going to Roundwood. Pat Whelan, now deceased, and myself visited the scene. It was a lonely stretch of road and at the time, there were no houses nearby. I don't know about now. A farmer, a young man, out checking his stock found her. She was facing upwards with a jacket thrown carelessly over the face. The image has always remained with me. There are some things that are never forgotten.'

Jack Lyons stopped for a moment to let a memory pass.

'There were two young gardaí there, when we arrived. We didn't touch anything. We just made sure that the integrity of the spot was not compromised.'

The old man paused again for a moment, this time to gather some breath.

'You could see the blood stains. I still see them, a dark red against a yellow top. It's such a pity that we got nobody for it.'

'Well,' Billy told the old copper, 'the case has been re-opened, new information has come to light. I'm sorry I can't say anymore, at least for the present.'

Jack Lyons nodded. He understood.

Ellie said nothing, he just watched Billy at work.

'Jack, can you remember what happened to the jacket?'

'It was looked after very carefully. We thought it might contain some evidence. It was taken back to the station, later sent to the lab for testing. I suppose it came back to Bray afterwards. I have no idea what happened to it but Molly Burke would know. That is if she is still with us.'

Nothing more came from old policeman but the two detectives stayed with him until he was called for his lunch. As they parted Billy promised to call another time. The old man nodded, not expecting to see these officers again.

Billy Lynch knew different.

Emer had decided that they were not going to travel far. Two days was far too short a time to spend hours in a car travelling to Kerry or the west. She had chosen Wexford.

It had taken only a couple of hours to get there and it had everything. The hotel was good and there was plenty to do.

A few pleasant walks, fine wine and some good food would recharge their batteries and eliminate the stresses of the previous weeks. They had made a pact that they would not talk business. The case would be parked in Dublin for the weekend. Emer knew that this had little chance of being adhered to but it had lasted until the Saturday afternoon.

'Do you think that we'll get him?' Harry asked as they sipped a couple of drinks.

Emer reckoned that they had done well to keep off the subject for almost twenty four hours.

'I don't really know,' she said, 'the motive seems logical but a defence mightn't find much difficulty in demolishing it in front of a jury.'

'Yes, I know what you mean. The theory that Hogan, in times of great political crisis, goes out and kills someone. It could be made to appear a bit far fetched.'

'You think Francis could be the perpetrator?' Emer asked.

'Or both of them?'

'You think that's a possibility?'

'No, not really. Hogan is the killer.'

And the two left it at that.

The pride of the county was playing poorly and Dan McCarthy knew it. He couldn't concentrate on his game. His concentration had been shredded and his attention was firmly focused on the sideline rather than on the goalposts. It was just as well that the match was only a friendly.

Ellie had decided to come to the game and to be his date at the dance but she had made clear it that there would be no strings attached. She had not noticed that her superstar colleague was not giving one of his vintage performances and if she had, Ellie Kennedy wouldn't have cared.

There was a jovial mood in the incident room on the Monday morning. Most had enjoyed the weekend break and were ready once again to strike a blow for law and order and to render unto Joanne Boylan a final gift, justice.

It was Billy who dispensed the news of Molly Burke. Harry had a vague memory of a middle aged woman who had worked around the station. He really had no idea how old she was, but as a young guard he had the impression that she was a woman in her middle years. The question was whether she was still living. If she was, maybe she could help them in their quest for the lost jacket. Her present status could easily be determined. The Bray station would certainly have a record of her.

Billy and Ellie were to continue the initiative and go to Bray to dig up what they could about Molly Burke.

As for himself, Harry needed to check on Michael Hutton's condition. He didn't expect much change. If there was a possibility that his health would improve and that he could make a statement, Harry wanted to know it. There was plenty of paper work to occupy Emer and Dan.

Then there was Mark Dowd. Harry wanted to talk to the solicitor again. It wasn't that he distrusted the veracity of his statement but he knew, from his years of experience, that there are details concealed in the memory that the individual may not recall easily. They will only surface by repeated visitations to the recollections of those events.

There was another issue that Tinto needed to address. How much longer could be spent delving into the past. He wasn't under any pressure to wrap things up but he was expected to realistically assess the chances of a positive conclusion and make a decision.

Harry set a deadline. Should there be no progress by Friday, the case would be closed for a second time. This time, it would be forever.

Billy and Ellie found Bray disappointing. Nobody had any recollection of a woman called Molly Burke. A reference to her existence was eventually found. It indicated that she had retired almost twenty years before. The record showed that she was sixty five years old at the time.

'That doesn't look good,' Ellie remarked. 'If she is still alive that would put her in her eighties.'

'And the chances of her recalling the jacket at her age is pretty slim. But, as Harry often says, one never knows.'

The station's records had no account of what had happened to Molly Burke afterwards. Her address, according to the officers, no longer existed. The house, with the others in the terrace where she had lived, had been demolished a decade before to make way for an apartment complex. But her social insurance number was there. Nowadays the number is referred to as PPS but the social welfare people would be able to track her down. If she was alive, she was being paid a pension and that would have an address linked to it.

The authorities in Bray Social Welfare were most helpful. It took them less than ten minutes to find an answer to the question. Yes, Molly Burke was alive and she was living in the old folks hospital in Ashford.

Ellie knew the hospital. Her grandmother had spent some time there. As she remembered it, it was a large establishment where many of its residents were confined to their beds.

A short phone call to the matron brightened all their days with the news that Molly was indeed with them and in good health. Harry would go along there in the afternoon and take Emer and Ellie with him. He would speak to the matron before deciding who would interview the old lady.

The squad car took the three gardaí up the drive to the main door of the hospital. They were expected and the matron, a Mrs. Dunlee, was there to greet them.

'Good afternoon Superintendent and ladies, you are very welcome. We would be pleased to assist you in any way we can.'

Harry thanked her and introduced his two colleagues. Then Mrs. Dunlee directed the three into a private sitting room. Tea and coffee were offered and Harry accepted the invitation for the three of them.

'Mrs. Dunlee, we are investigating a crime that was perpetrated in Bray some years ago and there is a possibility that Molly Burke might be in a position to assist us. At the time of the incident she worked in the local garda station and she might have some answers for us.'

'Molly would, I'm certain, be delighted to help you. She's totally reliable.' the matron replied.

'Would you think that Molly might be more comfortable with the two ladies interviewing her?' Harry asked.

Mrs. Dunlee laughed.

'With Molly, it's the more the merrier.'

With that the refreshments arrived and Mrs Dunlee departed to find Molly Burke.

As the gardaí waited, Harry noticed the tray had four settings, one for himself, one for Emer, one for Ellie and one for Molly. The gesture to include the old lady pleased him. It showed that respect and dignity for the aged, were alive and well and living in Ashford Hospital.

Molly Burke was a small wiry little woman with a receding hairline, a slightly stooped back and a very wide toothless smile. She was delighted with her three visitors and was not the least bit intimidated by their presence. After the introductions, Mrs. Dunlee discreetly withdrew to allow the police to get on with their work.

Harry expected that it might take some time to get to the hub of the matter. He had not wanted to rush matters but Molly got to the point immediately.

'How can I help you?'

'About thirty years ago a young girl was killed and her body dumped .....'

'You mean Joanne, she was a lovely girl.'

Harry was stunned. Not only was Molly alert and clear, it appeared she had known the victim.

'You knew her?' Harry asked.

'Oh yes, I knew her well, she lived on the same terrace as I did. It was such a pity you know. They never got anyone for doing her.'

'That's why we are here Molly. We are examining the case again and we need some help. There was something collected at the time that might help us catch her killer but we cannot find it. It was the jacket that had been thrown over Joanne. We're asking everyone who is still around and Jack Lyons mentioned you.'

'Jack Lyons, I remember him, nice man he was. How is he now?'

'He is in a wheel chair but is in good shape.' Ellie answered her.

'I remember the jacket, there was some dried blood on it. It was tweed and it looked expensive. I suppose it was with the other evidence.'

'What other evidence, Molly?' Harry interjected.

'I don't know, maybe Joanne's clothes.'

Harry could have kicked himself, it was such a basic issue. They had not even thought of the girl's clothing. And it had taken this alert old woman to remind them. Neither Emer or Ellie had noticed the significance of Molly's remarks but felt an intensity seeping from their boss as he continued the conversation.

'All the evidence was kept in a special store and nobody had keys except the bosses. They were always very careful with the stuff in that room.'

There was no more that Molly could add to the scenario but the three took their time before taking their leave. In the community of the hospital the three gardaí would have celebrity status and Molly Burke was in her element as she escorted her three guests back to the entrance and their car.

Harry was quiet on the way back to the station. It was not that he was disturbed but he didn't want to be overheard by the driver. However it did not inhibit him calling the incident room and arranging for everyone to be there when he got in.

'There's been a cock up.' Harry announced to his assembled team. 'We're all part of it but it is my error most of all. We have been searching for Hogan's jacket but we have neglected to consider Joanne Boylan's clothing. We presumed her clothing was returned to her family after the case was closed, just as was done with the other girls' effects. But Joanne Boylan had no family, there was nobody to give them to. So we are now looking for her clothes as well as the jacket. There could be DNA on her clothes just as there could be on the jacket.'

Harry let his point sink in before continuing.

'Another thing, we are coming close to the wire at this stage and we really have very little, other than Dowd's statement and Hutton's admissions to build a case on. So a decision on the future of the investigation is needed and I have made it. Unless we get somewhere before the weekend, we're going to throw in the towel. I know that you won't like doing this, neither will I, but a time always comes when the sun needs to set.'

Harry was right. The squad did not like the idea of walking away but they knew he was correct when he said that they did not have a viable case. However, there was still four and a half days to the weekend and as Dan knew the match was never won or lost until the final whistle was blown. He couldn't count the number of matches he had played that had been decided in the very last minutes of the joust.

Billy and Ellie had continued interviewing the old gardaí but there had been no breakthrough. The men had all been interested and willing to do what they could but they had nothing to add to the body of knowledge.

A phone call to the Mater Hospital confirmed that Pete Halpin had had his procedure carried out and was comfortable. That was all that they would say over the phone but it was enough.

Fiona and the baby, as a duet, were beginning to settle in with Harry but it was too early to say that they had formed a routine. However, even at this early stage, it looked like they could all live with the new regime. Of course, there were decisions that needed to be made and issues to be addressed such as what happens when Fiona's maternity leave was exhausted.

Harry was enjoying the baby. He knew his contribution to her daily well being was minimal but he was there, in the background, ready and ever willing to step into the breach if he was ever needed.

The weekend away had done him wonders. A weight seemed to have been lifted from his shoulders and although he was disappointed that the case seemed to be grinding to a halt, he knew that that happened and that there would be other cases. He would have liked to have succeeded this time. It was bad enough for a perpetrator to get away with murder once but four times made his heart sink.

Of course, Hogan, Francis and Dowd might not get away scot-free. They had been involved in the removal of Joanne Boylan's body so Harry had them on charges of accessory after the fact. Unless Dowd repudiated his statement he could still bring those charges.

Harry had wanted justice for all four girls and their families. He wanted the killer to be charged, convicted and sentenced for his crimes but that now seemed quite remote.

Harry had not finished with either Dennis Hogan or Peter Francis yet. The previous week's interview was just step one, the first kick of the last phase of the game. Harry would be meeting them both again. The second interview would be followed by the taking of a statement and this would formalise the procedure that they were undertaking. Hogan's denial of any involvement was to be expected but he had lied.

The privilege Hogan had been granted, in being allowed to be interviewed at his solicitor's rooms, would not recur. The next time they spoke would be in Store Street and although Harry would not encourage a leak to the press, he would do nothing this time to help shield the minister.

But certain proprieties needed to be observed. The principal one was to Taoiseach Matt Dolan.

The Taoiseach took Harry's call. It was brief and to the point. No names were mentioned and the gist of the conversation was that an individual would be taken in for questioning in the morning. He would be given the option of coming in voluntarily but if he refused, he would be arrested. Harry told Dolan that the case for murder had not, at this point, been established and now seemed remote. However, there was sufficient evidence to pursue a lesser but still very serious charge.

Matt Dolan thanked the Superintendent for the information. After he had replaced the phone, the Taoiseach realised that the more he dealt with Harry Tinto the greater the respect he had for the man.

Dolan was realistic enough to know that once Hogan was interviewed, it would not take long for the news to filter out into the public domain. There was nothing for him to do, but he would be questioned for a reaction and he knew what that would be. There would be no fulsome support for his old adversary and cabinet colleague. He would express some surprise and indicate that it was totally a matter for the police. They had a job to do.

Dennis Hogan was surprised when he got a call from Ellie Kennedy.

'Mr. Hogan, Superintendent Tinto wants to see you at Store Street at ten in the morning,' the garda said.

'It may not be convenient,' he replied irritably.

'Sir, this is not a request. He expects you to be there. The Superintendent said he could send a car.'

'OK, I get the message,' the politician said and hung up.

Hogan had got the message loud and clear. If he did not appear he would be arrested and taken into custody. The fat would surely be in the fire then. It was clear that Tinto was not satisfied with his version of events. More than that, the policeman clearly believed he was lying. Otherwise he would have shown more respect in the manner of the delivery of his demand.

There was work to be done, an attitude to determine and a decision to be made. He needed to limit the damage as much as possible.

There were a few absolutes. One was, that if word of him being a suspect became public knowledge, his ministerial career would be over. If he didn't resign then Dolan would fire him and the Taoiseach would not mourn his fall from grace. There were still a couple of years left to an election. If there was no conviction he might still survive as a parliamentarian, but that was a very big 'if'.

He needed to consult Maurice Brown.

There were aspects of the case that needed further thought and Harry took himself out to the park in Fairview to attempt to marshal his thoughts on the motive for the killings. As he had told his team, the motive that he ascribed to Hogan was not certain but he was still convinced by it. However if he was wrong, it left Hogan with no apparent motive for the killings.

There might be a simple logic to the motivation for three of the deaths. It may have been simply the urge for the taste of blood and the thrill of the kill, that had lead the killer down the highway of death that he had travelled.

If what he thought was true, the motive did not matter. What counted was who the killer was and he remembered that Hutton had said that Hogan had admitted the killing.

Even in the late autumn afternoon sunshine Harry could feel a gloom beginning to descend. But there were still some points to play for. They had forgotten about the girl's clothing, they had made a mistake and if they had erred, so too could others. He would organise another search for the missing jacket and this time he would include the girl's garments in the quest. It could do no harm.

Dennis Hogan would, he expected, be a tough nut to crack. Harry had no expectations of a confession or anything close to it but Hogan would feel the pressure. The ignominy of a ruined reputation and a period in jail might tempt him to try to salvage something. Hogan was certainly between a rock and a hard place. He was unaware of what the police could prove. The minister might speculate that the police had a lot. Then again the police might know a lot but could prove nothing. It was a question of risks and balances. Hogan would know that Hutton was out of action, so that left Mark Dowd and Peter Francis. He could count on Francis but not on Dowd.

Harry realised that what he had been doing was really just fantasizing. He had no way of knowing how the minister's mind worked.

Later when he returned to the station, he asked Billy to go to Bray and double check for the jacket and check if anything was known about the girl's garments. He was to take whoever he wished with him. Harry was not surprised when he took Ellie.

A few hours later, Billy rang in. Both Ellie and he had gone through everything they had in Bray and there was still no sign of Hogan's jacket. Nobody knew what had happened to Joanne Boylan's clothing.

The next morning Dennis Hogan arrived on time. Maurice Brown, his solicitor, was with him. This time Brown was not permitted to attend the questioning. The solicitor was not surprised when informed of his exclusion. Hogan, on the other hand, was seriously taken aback. Not only was he being interviewed in a garda station but he was being treated like any ordinary criminal. Tinto was making no allowances for his political importance and his clout in circles of power and influence.

He waited, seated at a table, in the interview room. Hogan pondered whether the Taoiseach had been informed and concluded that he had been.

There had been no phone call the previous night, so the conclusion that the minister had drawn was, that his old adversary had left him out to dry. There would be no support and no intervention. He was on his own, so if a deal was to be cut he would have to do it himself.

Harry took Billy with him on this occasion. This time he would require a statement at the end of the proceedings. The Superintendent began by cautioning the man opposite him after Billy switched on the recorder. The questions and the answers followed the same route as on the previous occasion. It was obvious that Hogan was sticking to his guns and admitting nothing. He knew nothing, according to himself, of Joanne Boylan or Angela Forde or Miriam Nolan. He did not remember July 10th 1977. Yes, he could have been drinking in the International Hotel but he didn't help anyone dispose of a body and he certainly didn't kill anyone.

The interrogation continued in this vein for some hours with Harry making no breakthrough. Hogan was good and was not making any mistakes. There were no serious contradictions with what he had said previously.

Eventually it was over. All that remained was the statement and that would take another few hours but Harry would leave that to Billy, Emer and Dan.

After Harry emerged from the interview, he felt a buzz of excitement around the place. Another ten seconds told him what was afoot. The press had got wind of the presence of the minister in the station. The hacks smelled a story and like hounds they were baying to be the first to find out what was going on.

Harry knew the truth was of no consequence for some newspapers. If the story wasn't the dynamite they hoped for, they could always dress it up.

It was time to have a word with the Chief Superintendent. Donal Joyce would want to be updated if a government minister was in his station for questioning.

'What's going on, Harry?' Joyce asked before Tinto had a chance to seat himself.

'Dennis Hogan is downstairs. I brought him in for questioning. He is making a statement at the moment. I guess our friends in the press have heard about it.'

'Did you get anywhere with him?'

'No, it's almost the last throw of the dice. We know that Hogan is guilty of murder but we cannot build a murder prosecution against him. I think we might get Hogan, Francis and Dowd for being accessories but that's the best there is.'

'Do you think the DPP will run with it?' Joyce asked

'I'm not sure he will.'

Donal Joyce shook his head. He too, would have liked this case to come to a positive conclusion.

'How long more will you give it, Harry?'

I want to talk to Francis once more, probably tomorrow. If we get nothing more, we'll close down on Friday. Donal, I really wanted to clear this one up but you win some and you lose some.'

The evening television and radio news bulletins were full of the minister's visit to Store Street. Hogan had spoken to the assembled media on his way out. He played down the whole event. He couldn't tell what was involved because of the sub-judice rules but he could say that it related to an incident that occurred during his student days. He had not been involved in this incident but the police thought that he might be aware of something that might help them in their inquiries. Unfortunately, he had been of no assistance to them.'

After work Harry and Emer were together in Baker's lounge.

'It's a long time since yesterday,' Harry remarked, 'I always get a bit downbeat when I have to throw in the towel. I told Joyce that Friday was the deadline and after that we go with what we have.'

'What do you mean?' Emer asked.

'There will be no murder charge but I think there might be enough to prefer charges relating to the disposal of the body and concealing information about a crime,' he replied, 'but it'll be up to the DPP to decide.'

'How will he see it? Will he be influenced by Hogan's high profile and political standing?'

'I don't believe that it will be a factor. However if Hogan and Francis are charged, the DPP will also have to charge Dowd and Hutton. All we have is Dowd's admission to his own involvement and his implication of the other three. There is, of course, the possibility that Hutton might be well enough to corroborate Dowd's statement but I wouldn't rely on that. The downside from the DPP's point of view is, of course, the length of time that has elapsed since the killing.'

'You think that they could walk away from all of this unscathed?' Emer asked.

'Yes, it's certainly a possibility,' Harry replied.

Sometime later when Harry reached his front door he was taken a bit by surprise. There, Sellotaped to the letter box, was a message for him.

'Please Dad, no noise and don't bang the door. Monica is sleeping.'

So following instructions Harry Tinto crept silently into his home and, for the first time in more than two decades, he disturbed nobody. Then peering round the door of his living room, he saw his granddaughter and daughter both lost in a world of sleep. He enjoyed the moment and leaving them to their dreams, retreated to the kitchen for a glass of red wine.

As he sat with his drink, his mind returned to the vision he had encountered in his front room. Life, for a single mother, he thought, must be very difficult. Fiona would be alone a lot of the time. There was little respite. There was nobody to the share the responsibilities and challenges, the joys and the sorrows of rearing a child. It must, Harry concluded be a very lonely life. His hope would be that Fiona would someday find someone, who would love her and her baby and cherish and look after them both.

Emer had a surprise waiting for her when she reached her house. The front door was open, the lights were on and the sound of music was coming to her loud and clear. Someone had come home.

13

The air of gloom, that Harry had sensed the day before, seemed to have descended on the incident room and its occupants the next morning. They were at a standstill. All the avenues of the investigation had been faced and nothing remained. The long shots had produced nothing. As Billy reported the previous afternoon there was no luck with the jacket and the victim's clothing in Bray.

There was still a job to be done. A file needed to be prepared to be sent to the DPP for charges against all four living participants, in the removal of the body of Joanne Boylan to the ditch in the Wicklow hills. The DPP might decide differently but his rejection would not be due to sloppy work by Tinto's crew. And, of course, there was Peter Francis to be re-interviewed.

Francis had given nothing away during their previous encounter and unless something had changed, that Harry was unaware of, nothing of substance would come from this interview either.

Harry started at the beginning but the responses were almost identical to the last time he had interviewed Francis and so it continued. But the policeman would not let go.

There was a knock on the interview room door and Ellie Kennedy entered and handed Harry a note. Interrupting the interview for some minutes Harry left the room.

'Michael Hutton has had a second stroke. He died thirty minutes ago.' Ellie told her boss.

'Thanks Ellie,' Harry said and returned to his interview.

He knew the game was surely up at this point. Francis and Hogan wouldn't budge and with Hutton now deceased, Mark Dowd was certain to attempt to repudiate the statement he had made earlier. Everything was gone, there was no possibility that the three would be asked to account for their actions, in a court of law. Hogan and Francis would be free and justice would again be denied to the four girls.

Francis had sensed that the news that Harry had received had not been good. The policeman had lost much of his vigour and now Peter Francis, sensing victory, was more macho than ever.

That afternoon, Harry stopped the work on the file. There was no point. As long as Michael Hutton was alive, Dowd would have played ball. Now that the teacher was dead, the game was over.

Harry expected to hear from Dowd, probably through his lawyers, complaining about the methods used to get the statement. It would all be rubbish, of course, but it would be their justification for rejecting Dowd's statement as being legally unsound.

There was nowhere to go. Harry told everyone to go home early. He didn't expect that any of them would enjoy the afternoon off but being away from the station would help them to accept that all cases, like all love stories, don't have happy endings.

As for himself, a trip down to Greystones on the DART and a walk along the sea front would remove the cobwebs that had re-appeared in the previous few hours.

Dan and Ellie decided to spend the afternoon together. They thought that a short visit to the Mater Hospital to look in on Pete Halpin would be nice. Then afterwards, maybe they would go to a movie together.

Emer's surprise guests the previous night had been her son Brian and his partner Michael. She was getting used to their relationship by now and was glad to see them. They were going to stay with her for a few days before travelling down to Athlone to meet Billy's parents. They were, like Emer had been, in the dark about their son's sexual orientation and now both men had decided it was time to be open with them about their relationship.

However, that evening they were taking Emer out to dinner and now there was time for her to get her hair done.

143

This was not the first time that Harry Tinto had failed to catch his prey. He knew the disappointment would soon pass. But there was an aspect to this failure that was causing him some anxiety. It was the possibility that the killer might strike again.

Harry returned to the incident room and as he had expected, there was nobody there. Sitting at his desk he noticed a sealed envelope addressed to him. Opening it, he found an epistle from Mark Dowd's solicitor. It was, as he had anticipated, the first step in Dowd's repudiation of his signed statement. The cover letter informed Tinto that Dowd was now under medical supervision and that access to him would now occur, only with the approval of his medics.

The letter did not mention the statement Dowd had made but Harry knew that it was only a matter of time before its admissibility was questioned.

For the next few minutes Harry did nothing. Looking at the answering machine he noted that there were five messages. Switching on the machine, he listened. The first three messages were for the others. The remaining two were from Mrs Dunlee, the matron, in Ashford Hospital. She asked, on both occasions, for Harry to give her a call.

Harry dialled the hospital and was put through to Mrs Dunlee directly.

'Superintendent,' she began, 'thank you for calling me, it's about Molly Burke. Since your visit she has been very quiet, thoughtful might more accurately describe her mood. As you can understand, older people have good days and bad days. Today this thoughtfulness turned to anxiety and all she wanted was to see you. We asked her why but all she would say was 'I want to talk to the Superintendent.' What I'm asking is that you might phone her, and talk to her. It would ease her mind.'

'That's no problem. Would around eight o'clock be suitable?' Harry asked.

'That would be perfect.'

Suddenly Harry changed his mind.

'Mrs. Dunlee, change of plan. I'll call to see her instead. Would the same time be ok?'

The matron was pleased that Harry would visit. It would do much to lift the dark clouds that hung over a nice old lady's day.

Harry had no commitments for the evening. He knew that his presence was not required at home. The girls plus one small baby had plans. Emer was having dinner with Brian and his partner, so what better way to spend a fine autumnal evening than a drive down to Wicklow. He would enjoy a meal in some tavern along the way. It would be all to the good if a little of his time would help a grand old lady jettison some of a burden that she carried on her now stooped and tired shoulders.

Anne Dunlee was waiting for Harry and as before, she ushered him into the same sitting room.

'I told Molly you were coming and you have no idea how it calmed her. It was kind of you to come all this way.'

'Not at all, it was a nice drive and, in truth, I had a free evening,' Harry replied.

The matron left to find Molly but was back within a minute. Molly had been watching out for the Superintendent and was waiting down the corridor.

The old woman seated herself opposite the policeman and waited until the matron had left the room.

Harry noted immediately that there was nothing wrong with Molly Burke. There was nothing feebleminded about her. She was alert and in control and she certainly had something to say.

'Superintendent, when you were here the other day you asked me about the jacket that had been thrown over poor Joanne's face. You said that you couldn't find it or any of her clothes. You said that they were missing and I wasn't able to help you.'

Harry said nothing letting her take her time to tell her story.

Molly continued.

'It bothered me. In all the years I spent in the Bray station I have never known anything important to get lost. The guards were always so careful with evidence and such things. This got me thinking and last night I woke up in the middle of the night and I remembered.'

'Remembered what?' Harry prompted.

'I remembered the renovations,' Molly answered. 'A few years before I retired the whole station was redone. A big extension was added and the old building was re-decorated and modernised. It took almost a year and during that time much of the garda work was done from temporary prefabs in the grounds. Now, what I think might interest you Superintendent, is that a lot of the stuff that was not needed was stored in the attic of the old station for safekeeping. As far as I can remember, only what was needed, was taken down. Joanne's things might still be there.'

Molly Burke had finished. She was smiling broadly.

So was Harry Tinto.

As he drove back, Harry had the feeling of euphoria. An opening had appeared at the end of the cul de sac. Harry had to keep reminding himself that, in the morning, all he might find facing him was another closed door. On the other hand he was reminded of the saying that the song is never over until the very last note has been sung.

A phone call to Billy found an answering machine and he left a message asking his friend to meet him in Bray, at the Garda station at nine o'clock.

Tinto didn't say why.

Billy Lynch was waiting for Harry from eight thirty. He was perplexed. He had believed, like the others, that it was all over and there was nowhere else to go. But Harry must have something up his sleeve.

Just before nine, Harry arrived.

'Billy, it's not over, not yet anyhow. You remember the name Jack Lyons gave you, Molly Burke. As you know, Emer, Ellie and I visited her last week and found a nice old woman and nothing else. Well, I got a message saying she wanted to see me so I dropped down to Ashford last night. She has given us one last kick of the ball.'

'A little like Dan in the All Ireland,' Billy remarked.

'Yes, just like Dan, only we don't know yet if there's a score. Molly remembered that in the early nineties there was a major refurbishment of the station in Bray and for the duration of the work, a large quantity of dead files and materials were stored in the attic of the old building for safekeeping. She thinks much of it remained there.'

'You think the jacket and the clothes are there still, Harry?' Billy asked.

'I don't know but that's what you and I are here to find out.'

It took ten minutes to get a search of the attic organised. It was a job for younger limbs than those of the two detectives from Store

146

Street. Molly had been right. There was a lot of material still stored there. The boxes were sealed and identified with a name written across the side. There were two boxes which carried the name Joanne Boylan. The young officers took those boxes from their resting place and brought them down.

Harry was given a small room to open the boxes and examine their contents. It was with some trepidation that Superintendent Tinto removed the tape that sealed the first. There were three questions in his mind and the first one would be answered in a moment.

Opening the lid, he saw, packed in a protective bag, a man's tweed jacket. He didn't touch anything. Then turning to Billy he said simply.

'The jacket, we have it.'

'Bloody hell,' was all Billy could say.

Then Harry removed the seal on the second box and lifted the lid. Again packed in protective bags were Joanne Boylan's clothes.

After a few moments of relief, it was back to business. There was no way that Harry wanted the integrity of this evidence to be compromised. All care was to be taken with it until the arrival of the Technical Bureau. Nobody was to touch anything.

'Billy, I want you to stay with this stuff until the guys from the bureau arrive. If you need a coffee, forget it.'

And then he was gone.

As he drove back into Dublin, he pondered about the difference a day makes. The two remaining questions he had in mind came back to him. Was there DNA on the jacket and on the girl's clothing?

His last question was whether they would get a DNA match?

'We're a lot closer than we've ever been.' Harry said aloud to himself.

The remainder of the squad was wondering about the whereabouts of their boss when Superintendent Harry Tinto walked back in. There was such a lightness in his step that his walk could have been mistaken for a dance. He reminded Dan of an old English teacher he once had.

'We're back in business, we've got the jacket and the victim's clothes,' he announced.

There was a surge of emotion in the incident room and Harry outlined the train of events that had led to the discovery.

'We're not there yet, not until we get a DNA match. I don't know whether there is any DNA on the jacket. I don't know much about such things, maybe it has disappeared or evaporated.' Harry suggested.

'That doesn't happen with DNA, it's there forever,' said the voice of Ellie Kennedy from behind.

'Well, that's a huge relief,' Harry said appreciatively.

'Dan and Ellie, I want both of you to get our three friends back in. We need to get samples for the DNA analysis from Hogan and Francis. No word about the clothes or the jacket. If they want their solicitors with them it's ok. We've already got a sample from Dowd, I just want to talk to him.'

Harry was finished.

Then there was a quick call to Donal Joyce.

'Donal, we've got the jacket and the clothes.'

That afternoon there was little happening around the incident room. Matters were now out of their hands and there was little to be done but to wait for the technical results. The success of all their efforts over the last weeks rested on those results.

Dan and Ellie had located both Hogan and Francis and arranged for a sample to be taken. They hoped it would produce a match with DNA found on Joanne's clothing and of course, on the tweed jacket.

There had been no direct contact made with Dowd but his solicitor had informed them that, subject to medical approval, he would be available in the morning.

Harry had slipped away for a while. He had gone to the Mater hospital to look in on Pete. His colleague seemed to be in poor spirits. Pete was absorbed in his own difficulties and really didn't hear Harry when he told him how the case was progressing.

Emer had found something to do. If the technical reports were positive then a file would be needed to be sent to the DPP. So she started organising all the data gathered by the squad to date. She was happy doing this. Organisation and administration had been her forte throughout her garda career and she was pleased to be using her well honed skills in an area that might lead to the prosecution of the decade.

Ellie and Dan felt like loose limbs. There was nothing for them to do, so they retreated to the station canteen for coffee. Billy had just disappeared.

The fifteen mile trip to the Blue Haven retirement home in Bray took Billy a little under forty minutes. He had made a promise to an old policeman and he was not about to renege on his commitment. Jack Lyons was delighted to see the detective and for an hour they talked about the case of Joanne Boylan and the critical point that the investigation had now reached.

The DNA analysis would take time and there was nothing for it but to wait. There was still a little more that Harry could do. He was confident that if the tests were positive that there would be enough evidence to get Hogan, Francis and Dowd convicted of being accessories but it was always good to have something extra to back up a case. Dowd could still provide this insurance.

Harry was certain that Dowd, since Hutton's death, was playing games. The solicitor was setting a scene where he might be able to repudiate the statement he had made earlier. So far, he had said nothing.

Mark Dowd was no friend of Hogan's and his motivation was aimed solely at self preservation. Harry felt that he could still have him on his side. Should the solicitor's DNA prove to be present on the clothing, then everything would change for Mark Dowd. It could be suggested to him that if he supported the state's case there was the certainty that whatever punishments were given, his would be less. He might not escape a custodial sentence but it could be a greatly reduced one.

Mark Dowd presented himself with his solicitor at the station at ten o'clock the next morning. Harry was waiting and asked Dowd and his solicitor to follow him. He led them both to an interview room and all three sat down.

'Note,' Harry began, 'no caution, no recording. I suggest you say nothing, just listen.'

The two looked at Harry Tinto cautiously.

'Mr. Dowd, I have noticed your changed attitude to the investigation since Michael Hutton's death. It would be my guess that you plan to repudiate your statement. However, it is my experience that important decisions that could have a traumatic effect on a person's life should not be made until such time as the individual is cognisant of all the relevant information.'

Harry stopped momentarily but the two facing him said nothing. They knew the Superintendent was not finished.

'In the present instance, Mr. Dowd, you are already aware that the jacket thrown over the girl, when she was laid out in the ditch, has been located. So too has all her clothing. These items, as you might guess, have been sent for DNA analysis. Of course, we have no results yet. I just thought you might like to know this.'

Harry stopped and then added.

'You are now free to go, Mr. Dowd.'

Dowd nodded to Harry as the detective left the room. The solicitor knew what he was being told and the implications it might have for his future.

Some days later the results of the DNA analysis were back. They showed that the tweed jacket contained only Dennis Hogan's and Mark Dowd's DNA. However, the girl's outer clothing contained significant DNA from Hogan, Francis, Dowd and others. Harry presumed that Martin Devereaux's and Hutton's DNA were there as well but the lab had nothing to match it with.

Harry was now in a position to prefer charges. There wasn't sufficient evidence to get a conviction for murder but there was certainly enough to charge all three with being accessories to murder. As Harry had expected, Mark Dowd had not repudiated his original statement. He would stand by what he said. There would be an enormous cost for his student days' indiscretion but a girl had died.

Harry wondered whether there was still a chance to convict Dennis Hogan for murder. It all depended on a balance between loyalty and self preservation. The detective wondered what cost Peter Francis was prepared to pay to protect his friend. With the results of the DNA analysis available there was a chance that Francis might see where his best interests lay and testify against the minister. Harry would bring Peter Francis in, for questioning, one last time.

Dan and Ellie made the arrest. Francis was taken from his home and brought to Store Street station in a squad car. Francis was in shock. He could see the world, as he knew it, collapsing all around him. He was in a dark place and the preferment of the accessory to

150

murder charge deepened his gloom. When the formalities were completed, Peter Francis was installed in a cell to await the arrival of his solicitor.

Billy switched on the recorders. There were four people in the interview room. Harry wanted Francis's solicitor to be present at the interview.

'Mr. Francis,' Harry began, 'I don't want you to say anything for the present. Just listen to what I'm saying.'

Peter Francis nodded.

'When Joanne Boylan died, five men were involved in the removal of her body to a ditch on the road to Roundwood. There was Devereaux, Hogan, Dowd, Hutton and you. You have already made a statement where you stated that you had nothing to do with the incident. You were lying. Mark Dowd has made a statement which fully implicates you in the crime. In court, you might say, your defence could argue that Dowd is lying or mistaken.'

Francis was looking cautiously at Harry Tinto.

'You have stated as well, that you didn't know the girl, that you had never met her.'

Francis was nodding his head.

'How then has a significant amount of your DNA been found on the girl's clothing? How did it get there? Have you an explanation for this?

Harry stopped for a moment to let his words sink in.

'One thing you know now is that this is not a game. You have been charged with being an accessory to the murder of Joanne Boylan, so too, has Mark Dowd. Your lawyers will confirm that in these circumstances, a double digit custodial sentence is a probability. With full remission you will serve eight or nine years. It's a very long time.'

Harry paused for a moment and then continued.

'There are, I believe, two questions you need to ask yourself? Why should you continue to protect a man who has killed four times? And what benefit is there in that for you or your family? Remember, you didn't kill anyone.'

Tinto paused again.

Peter Francis said nothing.

Then Harry continued.

'There will be no deal. You have been charged, you will be tried and you will be sentenced. However, the judge, in determining your sentence, will take into consideration whether you have helped or hampered this investigation. For the moment I will leave it at that. Mr. Francis, you and your solicitor have much to consider, so I will leave you to your deliberations.'

Harry indicated to Billy that they had finished and after switching off the recorder, they left the room.

It was all over.

Francis had seen the sense behind Harry's monologue. He was going to save his own skin and throw his friend to the wolves. Why should he stick by Hogan? Francis believed that he hadn't harmed anybody. But he had. If Francis and the others had not shielded Dennis Hogan, then three other girls would not have died.

Peter Francis turned state's evidence and provided the prosecution with the means to charge Dennis Hogan with the murder of Joanne Boylan. In his statement to the police he stated that Hogan had admitted killing Joanne Boylan when he opened the boot of the stolen car.

When confronted with questions on the deaths of Sarah Malone, Miriam Nolan and Angela Forde, Peter Francis was less certain. He said that he had suspected that it might be Hogan's work but it was only a suspicion.

It was all over. Nobody would be charged with the murders of the girls from Cork, Limerick and Galway. The charge that Hogan would have to answer for was not all that Harry Tinto had wanted but it was all there would be.

EPILOGUE

On a cold and sunny February afternoon Harry Tinto stood, for a few moments, on the steps of the Four Courts. He was alone. The trial was over. The evidence against Dennis Hogan had been presented to the court and a jury of the politician's peers had found the former minister guilty of the murder of Joanne Boylan.

The judge had sentenced Hogan to life imprisonment. He would serve about twelve years. Dennis Hogan would be an old man when he was released. He had said nothing.

A few weeks later, Dowd and Francis had pleaded guilty to their involvement in the disposal of Joanne Boylan's body. Harry Tinto had told the court of their contribution to the investigation and the judge had taken the detective's comments on board. Both men were sentenced to five years imprisonment but Judge Kevin Martin suspended all of it. They would serve no time. However, with their glittering lifestyles now in tatters, they had paid an enormous price for their youthful wrongdoing.

Harry still regretted that Hogan had not answered for the deaths of Angela Forde, Sarah Malone and Miriam Nolan. However, the conviction and imprisonment of their killer had, Harry felt, provided a kind of justice for them. Maybe now, after so many years, the four young women might find a peace.

Justice is a curious thing, Harry thought. It means that people must be accountable for their actions. Harry Tinto knew that providing justice for a victim requires intelligence, hard work, experience and occasionally a little bit of luck. Harry knew that, in the case of Joanne Boylan, that morsel of good fortune had a name.

And that name was Molly Burke.

Lightning Source UK Ltd.
Milton Keynes UK
UKOW050829081111

181691UK00001B/7/P